Chthonian Dragons

By Matt Kirkby

· Chapter One

"So thou would claim that this is the egg of a demon?"

"Aye, my Lord Mage." The narrow-faced man ducked his head, then brushed lanky hair away from his face. "I would not lie to thee." He lifted his eyes up boldly, taking the opportunity to look around Conrad's study. In this room, the stone walls of the mage's tower were hidden by wood panels—the light-coloured wood carved and patterned with arcane sigils and exotic animals. Shelves hid most of the walls, laden with chests and pottery jars in addition to the trappings one expected to find around a man versed in the magical arts.

"Thou claim to me that this is the egg of a demon." The silver-haired mage repeated his statement.

"Aye, my Lord Mage," the traveller repeated. He had the cowl of his worn grey cloak pushed back.

The mage lifted his eyes from their study of the leathery object and peered across the timeworn oak table towards his visitor. The torches in their wall sconces flared more brightly for a moment. "The egg of a demon is truly a most rare and precious object...and thou have brought this most rare and precious object to me?" he asked, this time with confusion colouring his voice. The pinkish-grey surface of the leathery egg seemed to pulsate slowly, almost hypnotically as he ran his hands across it. It felt vaguely warm to his fingertips.

The other man nodded. "From a very great distance, Mage Conrad, and through many terrible perils." His red tunic and drab brown breeches were travel-stained and he smelled strongly of horse. "I knew that thou would be interested in such a priceless treasure. There has been talk throughout the barony about thy interest in matters, shall we say, 'beyond the normal sphere'?"

"There is always talk, Goodman Rolf." Conrad returned his gaze to the supposed egg. "Some men have too much time on their hands and chatter endlessly when silence would flow better from their tongues."

"Mages incite talk. Being a man of business, I make it a habit to know the wants and desires of potential clients." Rolf rubbed at the side of his overly-large nose and offered a toothless smile. "And mages are always interested in rarities such as this." He waved his hand at the tabletop. "And you do seem to have such an interest." He waved his right hand again, this time to indicate the furnishings of the tower room.

Conrad accepted the point. The walls of his office were laden with shelves filled with many strange and exotic curiosities—books filled with arcane lore, weapons taken from goblins, the skull of a Minotaur. "Oh, I must admit to being very much interested in a prize such as this...but why offer it to *me*?" His eyes narrowed. "Why not take it to the College?"

Rolf shook his head and offered a depreciating smile. "Because the mages there would likely not welcome me as openly as thyself. They would take this prize from me and use it for their own gain without offer of payment for my journeying across the length of this land. Thou, Conrad, I can trust to be honest."

"Honesty is overrated."

"Perhaps."

Conrad frowned and the room was silent for a long moment.

Rolf took the opportunity to look around again. *What could be inside those chests?* He could not help but wonder. *Oh, for but a few minutes alone in this place. I could be wealthy!* Or dead...mages were not easily robbed after all. He stared at a stuffed bird—it was green with yellow feathers that shimmered metallically in the flickering torchlight—which suddenly turned to look at him with bright eyes.

"Very well." The mage pulled a small leather pouch from inside one of the ornately carved chests on the floor beside his table. "Take it."

Rolf loosened the drawstrings so that he could open the pouch and look inside. "Thou are a man most generous," he replied after hastily cinching it closed again. The gemstones had sparkled in the torchlight.

"Most generous indeed." He slipped the worn leather pouch under his red tunic.

"There should be enough gems there to keep even thou happy. Now go, my apprentice will see thee out." He waved a hand in a negligent gesture, his green sleeve flapping as he did so.

Rolf rose smoothly to his feet and offered a low bow, giving his grey cloak a bit of a showy flourish. "A pleasure doing business with thee, Master Conrad."

"Indeed." The mage was staring at the egg, his guest already forgotten.

*　*　*

"For all the warmth of the night, it should be storming, a tempest sent by the Gods to blow away corruption from the capitol." Josem spoke aloud, his words lost in the murmuring of people praying and the other background noises of the Temple. His orange and red robes rustled as he walked.

"Josem, there are times that you lack compassion."

"Aye, Revered One, I have been told such before." Josem held out a burning splint of wood to light a beeswax candle with the flame from another already alight. The candle was a warm green colour. "The causes of temptation are too many and we are too few." He lifted his eyes.

The warm candlelight bathed the carved jade statues atop their marble pillars. The gold and jewels decorating the Gods glinted and shimmered while their expressions seemed to change every other second.

"There is a darkness coming."

"I have felt the taint in the air, Revered One." Josem turned to the Temple's most ancient priest.

Bells in one of the dozens of steeples chimed as the wind caught them.

"I feel at peace when I hear that sound." The Revered One's white beard hung well past his waist, with tiny bells woven into it. They made soft chimes and tinkles as he walked.

"Do ye?" Josem wore no bells as yet. *Save for festivals and rituals,* he amended. *'Tis not my place to wear such until the Gods deem me worthy.* "Many feel at peace with the music of the bells."

"It is the music of the Gods themselves." No mortal hands drew such sounds from the bells after all. "The Gods themselves play such melodies as they choose. Never do they play the same song twice." The Revered One walked along the marble tiled corridor with slow steps. "I hear the sweet strains of the music and I see the beauty of the Temple—the fluted columns, the gilded lanterns, the stained glass windows and ceilings—and I am hard-pressed not to weep at such beauty."

"I look at the corruption of the city and I weep."

"It is not so bad as thou believe, Josem."

"Perhaps thou travel along different streets than I, Revered One."

"I walk the world and visit its people...as do thee."

Josem bowed to a trio of acolytes as they passed by. The trio bowed back with deeper bows. None of them wore bells either.

"And yet," the Revered One said as they resumed their casual stroll, "like thee, I can feel a shadow against the sun's light." His voice had grown troubled. "There is an unseasonable chill in the air."

"A woman's voice on the wind?"

"Aye." The Revered One's wrinkled face shifted into a frown. The bells in his beard tinkled as he turned his head to look at the younger priest. "Ye have heard the mother crying?"

"In my dreams...just in my dreams, Revered One." Josem shrugged, uncomfortable with the abrupt turn in the conversation. "I have never seen my mother. I was given to the Temple the very day I was born."

"Many have tread that path as ye have done."

"I have no regrets. The Gods called to me from the youngest age, as they must have called to my mother. I go whence I am summoned."

"That is good." The Revered One took a few more steps. "There is a cult gathering strength in the poorer districts of the city. It appeals to many who are of weak minds and limited will."

"I have heard mention of this. The claim is that all should heed the call of the Mother." He grimaced.

"This new 'Mother' gains converts daily."

"I will look into it, if thou wish it?"

"I do." Distant voices rose in a song of prayer. "I do wish it, Josem."

· **Chapter Two**

"Planning on going to the Western Islands? Are thou Gods-touched?"

Mikel slowly lowered his mug and wiped foam from his mouth. "What do thou mean?" His dark brown eyes narrowed as he studied the man who questioned him. *Bold words for a ragged traveller,* he thought. He did not even notice the barmaid who hurriedly stepped away from the table and vanished into the crowded tavern.

The other man wore a red tunic and mud-splattered boots. He shook his own head in disbelief and pushed back the cowl of his grey cloak until it rested on his shoulders. "Surely thou have heard the tales?" He looked at the seated man, pausing long enough to brush greasy black hair away from his face.

"Of course I've heard the tales. I'm going there, aren't I?" Mikel leaned back in his chair. None of the other patrons in the crowded tavern seemed to paying attention to their conversation.

"Well, if ye wish to die then..."

"I have no plans to die on this adventure."

"No doubt words spoken bravely by many before thee." The man plopped himself down into one of the empty chairs at the knife-scarred table. "For centuries, the bravest adventurers throughout the baronies have sought to win glory by seeking to visit the Western Islands."

Mikel nodded and reached for his mug of ale.

"The western islands were once the heart of the great Nostronomun Empire."

"Yes, the greatest Human Empire in the world." Mikel nodded as all the old stories flashed through his memory. "It was a civilization that we have yet to match. Wonders of magic were commonplace. The commoners were well-off and the nobility were rich beyond measure."

"Aye, 'tis good to have wealth." He drained his mug. "I need another drink." He waved sharply to a barmaid. "More ale, Masil!" he ordered loudly in a commanding tone. "My mug is dry."

"Thy coins are good," the blonde barmaid said as she brought another clay mug to the table, "and far better than thy manners, Rolf."

He gave her a leer. "Do thou sell thyself along with thy ale?" he asked.

"Thou cannot afford my price." Her pale yellow skirts flared as Masil turned on her heel and pushed back into the crowd around the bar.

Mikel's eyes had narrowed.

"So," Rolf continued after a long drink, "thy childhood was filled with tales of the mighty empire and their vast and uncounted wealth." He chuckled at that. "Then thou also know that the nobles grew vain and their mages grew careless. They opened a portal into the Infernal Plane and unleashed a plague of terrible demons. Those demons destroyed the Nostronomuns and their cities. There's naught left there now save time-worn ruins."

"And their treasures?"

"Possibly treasure, but not likely much."

"We shall see." Mikel smiled, more to himself than to the other man. "I plan to return with treasures such as the Royal Court has never seen."

"Thou be more the fool then." Rolf drained his mug and then gestured to the barmaid again. "Two more, Masil...one for me and one for my soon-to-be-dead friend." He laughed again.

"I'm not thy friend."

"No, but if thou go to the Islands thou *will* soon be dead." Rolf brushed hair from his eyes and rubbed at his overlarge nose. "The ruins are haunted still and the demons must grow restless after so many centuries."

At another table, a man in a ragged green tunic chuckled. "Aye, I've had such dreams as all of thee might never know," he said loudly. "The Mother embraces me and her voice sings me sweet lullabies."

The other people at the table shook their heads and laughed roughly.

"'Tis truth!" the man protested. "The Mother favours me."

"Take another drink!"

"Thou are dreaming."

The door to the tavern burst open and a trio of Dwarfs entered, calling for ale.

"The distant Islands are not to be travelled lightly," Rolf said softly. "They are far from deserted and dangers lurk there such as thou have never imagined."

Mikel downed a good portion of his latest drink, even before Masil had once again bounced her way back to the bar. "Thou seem well informed about the Islands."

"I have travelled much." Rolf offered a toothless smile. "I have seen many strange sights. I have heard many strange stories."

"Good for you. Someday I will have such stories to share. Good day to ye." Mikel stood up, adjusted his blue cloak around his shoulders, and then walked out of the tavern.

* * *

The grand marketplace was crowded—it was always crowded—and the handful of city Guardsmen on patrol simply observed the doings impassively.

"The marketplace grows bigger every year, Helga." The man shook his head.

"Aye, Franz." The seamstress shook her own head. Her long hair was worked into an intricate series of braids, coiled atop her head. "I can recall when the market was a third this size. I was just a girl then, apprenticed to Mother Christine. Seamstressing was all that I could manage. A plain girl from the farms, without family or kin here, without even two copper coins to rub together. Mother Christine took me in. Her eyesight was fading and she needed younger eyes to manage the fine embroidery and lace." There was lace at her cuffs and collar and embroidery on the hems of her gown and cloak.

Franz gently brushed grey locks away from her face. "That long ago?" he asked.

"That long and then some." She smiled warmly at him, noting how he towered over her. "And now every time I see you, it's just to mend thy tunic."

"I come more often than that."

"Thou were a rogue in thy youth. Ye have not changed."

"I hope not." Franz smiled at her, then sighed. "I must go. I am expected at the palace this night."

"Ah, spending time with thy high-born friends. Such a step up from what thy poor mother could muster. Running with street urchins and the like."

"I seldom ran with street urchins, Mother." Franz was smiling as he spoke. "And thou are one of the most renowned seamstresses in the city," he protested. "Nay! In entire the barony!"

"Not so loudly!" Helga hissed. "I don't want word to spread or I would have no peace. Bad enough that I have nobility to tailor for, I need not a horde of pretentious commoners showing up for the same fashions."

Franz chuckled. "Good day to ye, Mother."

"Be off with thou then. Leave me to my work." She shook her head, her grey braids swinging. "Working my poor old fingers to the bone while thou drink away our coin."

"Thou have coin enough to buy an entire tavern. Thou could retire now and live out the rest of thy days without raising a finger. Thou could hire thy own seamstress."

"Hush, lad. What would I do with my own seamstress? How many skirts does a woman need?" She shook her head. "Retire so that I may lounge about at my leisure? Aye, my son, I could do such...and be dead of boredom ere mid-summer's day. Is that what thou wish for me?"

Laughing to himself, Franz waved his farewell to her. He soon found himself pacing along one of the main streets. The cobblestones were smooth under his boots. He did not look out of place there, though often he only felt at ease while off adventuring in some dark forest or hiking through the distant mountains. His face was rugged and the clothes he wore were well made, but his cloak was weatherworn. He walked with one hand resting on the hilt of his sword.

The streets of the capitol were crowded with people, as they always were. Wagons rumbled along, pulled by teams of horses while the merchants sat beside their drivers and glared at the throng slowing their progress. Townsfolk moved, some darting briskly on errands, others leisurely wandering. Hawkers and peddlers carried trays or pushed small carts, crying the natures of their wares. Travellers bought from some, haggled with others, ignored still others. The air hummed with the energy of the bartering.

Franz stepped around two men haggling with a fishmonger.

"Come to Otto's Menagerie and thou will see such sights as will leave thee shaking for moons to come!" The man's deep voice boomed out, carrying through the din. He wore a richly embroidered coat and his eyes glinted. "We have fearsome beasts of legend to amaze thy eyes just waiting beyond the city walls...in our wagons."

Franz snorted at the hawker's words.

"Come, lad, and see a dragon."

Taken by surprise, Franz laughed aloud at the man. "Thou would have me believe that thou keep a caged dragon within thy wagons?" he asked.

"Aye, my Lord. I am Otto and the bulk of my menagerie waits beyond the walls. A handful of coppers, my Lord, and thou might venture within this house to sample but a tiny taste of the wonders I have gathered ere thou wander to my waiting wagons."

Franz frowned. "It is an unassuming house." It was a rather ramshackle inn from all looks.

"We could scarce bring the full menagerie within the city walls," Otto said, his lips twisting behind his long moustaches. "Herein lies but a sample. In our camp, thou will see the greatest wonders in the world."

"Including a dragon."

"Aye, including a mighty dragon." Otto had raised his voice and now his words echoed across the square, causing people to stop and look. "A most fearsome beast which we have safely caged."

"I have fought dragons...they would devour thee in an instant."

"I have raised this one from an egg." Otto looked around—making the gesture rather ostentatiously—then leaned towards Franz and lowered his voice to a soft whisper. "Tame as a housecat, she is."

Franz shook his head. "I have no coin to waste on such idle diversions as some fake dragon." He turned and took a step away. "But surely thou will find many fools here eager enough to give thou their money."

The hawker's voice rose again as he called to the crowds to behold his marvels for a few coppers.

Franz chuckled and walked.

"Thou are not taken in, Franz?"

Franz turned his head at the shout. "No, Josem, I am not."

The crowds parted for the priest as he strode towards the other man. His robes were of rich cloth, in the bright orange and red hues of his faith. "I am pleased to hear that." His pointed beard was neatly trimmed with a single bell tied to its tip.

"Are you?"

"The city is crowded with both liars and thieves." The priest stroked his chest-length black-and-white beard. "They prey upon the credulous with their most outlandish stories."

Franz glared at a young man who was reaching for his belt-pouch. The would-be pickpocket turned and hastily ran into the crowd. "The Guards grow lax it seems." His own beard was thick and dark, far more suited to a woodsman than to a courtier. *Would that I could be out adventuring more often than I am. The Court is too soft for my liking despite its own dangers. The perils here cannot be banished with a sword.*

"Temptation and false beliefs poison our souls. The Gods will turn their backs upon us for such foolishness." Josem was truly warming to his subject as he denounced the city and its habitants. His robes rustled.

"Nostronomun revisited?"

Josem glared at him. "Lessons once learned are being forgotten!" he snapped. "There are muggings and theft by day and debauchery, murder, and rapine by night."

"The City Guards—"

"Cannot be in every alley, nor at every corner."

"What would thou have me do?"

Josem smiled warmly. "Thou have the ear of the Baroness. A few words spoken softly to Carolinka might go a long way towards...*convincing* the faithful where their spiritual loyalties lay."

"I will do what I can, but I can make no promises."

"Of course, I quite understand."

"And the Mother has spoken to me!" A voice cut through the din. "She has whispered to me and commanded that I pass along her words to thou all."

"Ye Gods, another one." Josem groaned loudly.

"Another what?" Franz eyed the ragged-looking man. "Street beggars often harangue the crowds. Few listen these days."

"The latest cult." Josem shook his head with resignation and his bell chimed. "They are spreading through the poorer neighbourhoods like the Red Pox."

"What cult?"

"These deluded fools preach of their *Mother*." Josem grimaced. "Some supposed fertility goddess from the outer provinces. Nameless, faceless, simply called the 'Mother'. They preach of joining with her and bearing her young. Madness I tell you."

Franz nodded. "No doubt." His gaze moved back towards the speaker.

The man wore a ragged tunic and breeches that more holes than cloth. "I know that thou feel something lacking in thy lives. Thou feel emptiness. Despair not, for I have the answer! Thy emptiness will be filled!" the unkempt man shouted to the passers-by. "The Mother will fill thee with her love. Thou will be blessed and the glory of the Mother will fill thou and thou will be fulfilled as thou bear the sons and daughters of the Mother!"

"I can bear no more of this!" Josem strode forward, parting the standing people with a sweep of his staff. "*Falsehoods*!" he bellowed with all the righteous outrage that he could muster. "Spreader of lies! There is no 'Mother'! The true Gods will not long abide such wickedness from thy tongue!"

"Guard thy own tongue, Priest!" the man snarled back. "Thy false prophets and thy equally false gods have brought ruination to our realms."

Josem halted in mid-step, his brown eyes opening wide in shock.

Franz stared back as well. *No one talks like that to priest!* he thought. *Tis simply not done.* The marketplace was growing silent as more and more people turned their attention to the would-be preacher and the priest.

"Blasphemy!" Josem bellowed. "Thy words—"

"Thy false gods demand worship from afar," the preacher yelled back, "and despite sacrifices and offerings in thy temples, they remain silent and sterile! The Mother will touch thee! The Mother will join Herself with thee."

Josem's face was a bright red, rapidly turning purple.

"The Gods shelter and protect us!" someone shouted from amongst the listeners.

"Thou speak blasphemy!" added another man, faceless in the crowd.

"The Mother loves you!"

"The Gods love us."

"The Mother's love is less conditional and far more tangible. She reaches into thy dreams and fills thy soul with warmth."

Franz shook his head as a pair of Guardsmen came into view. "This can't end well."

The two Guards wore polished breastplates over their puffy-sleeved yellow coats, with conical helmets and silver-trimmed green cloaks.

"Do not allow thyselves to be misled!" the unkempt man raved. "The Mother will come among us, walk amongst us openly with her Children, and we will join with her in the most blessed of communions!"

"Delusional wretch!" Josem bellowed. "Thou rave of insanity."

"I speak the truth! The Mother is coming and only those who join with Her in communion will be saved when this barony is lashed with destruction!"

"Blasphemer!"

More Guardsmen were hurrying towards the argument.

· **Chapter Three**

Mikel strode through the corridors of the Palace, the heels of his boots ringing loudly on the marble-tiled floor. Armed sentries watched him pass, as warily as did servants and courtiers. No one spoke up as he hurried by.

"Bloody cowards," Mikel muttered to himself as he walked quickly enough to make his dark blue cloak billow out behind him. "Afraid to even make eye contact." He snorted.

A maid almost dropped the armload of linens she was carrying.

Mikel looked at her. "What?" he growled.

The maid turned and fled.

With another snort, Mikel stomped past a tapestry depicting some ancient and otherwise forgotten battle. There were numerous windows here, allowing sunlight to flood the corridors and hallways.

A figure moved past the next corridor.

Mikel increased his pace. "Franz!"

"Aye?" The older man turned. He was weathered and rugged in appearance, as befitted a man who spent most of the year out-of-doors. His black tunic, brown breeches, and grey cloak were serviceable though drab and thoroughly out-of-place for the palace.

"I gave orders to have my horse saddled and waiting this morning. Thou countermanded me!"

"Did I?"

"Thou hid my horse!"

Franz smiled, his teeth white against his dark beard. "I didn't want to risk thou leaving without me." He rested his left hand on the sword sheathed at his waist.

"As if I would." With a grin, Mikel slapped him on the back. "But why hide my horse?"

Franz shrugged. "That was not *my* doing. My steed is also missing. It seems that the Baroness has hidden both of our horses, according to the stable master."

Mikel grimaced. "Damned woman." His fingers tightened around the hilt of his own sword. "So where is the bitch?"

Franz winced at both his words and tone. "Waiting in her throne room no doubt."

Mikel nodded. "Come on then. Let's go and see what she wants this time." He stalked off, his dark blue cloak billowing behind him once again.

* * *

Mikel stormed through the corridors, Franz following in his wake.

Two guardsmen stood outside the doors to the throne room. They both wore full armour, their breastplates and helmets polished until they shone like mirrors. Their helms were ornate and patterned like pine branches, the metalwork masking their faces. Beneath their armour, both men wore green coats with puffy yellow sleeves, with green breeches and black boots.

Mikel stopped in front of the doors. The doors were impressive—twice the height of a man, and sheathed in copper. A stylized oak tree had been engraved into the copper.

Franz brushed lint from his tunic. "We wish entry."

"The Baroness is holding court."

Mikel looked at the man who had spoken. "She *will* see us."

The guard opened his mouth to say something.

Mikel drew his sword in an instant and placed its tip against the guard's throat. "She will see us," he growled.

The other man-at-arms half-drew his own sword, but Franz lifted his hand and shook his head. "Franz, this will accomplish nothing. The poor man is only doing his duty."

With a muttered curse, Mikel violently sheathed his sword.

Franz pasted a soothing smile onto his face. "We are both summoned to an audience with the Baroness."

The sentries exchanged looks.

"Do ye doubt my words?"

"No, my Lord," the man replied, clearly eying Franz's clothing. "But we have had no word about expecting you."

The doors swung outwards, on well-oiled hinges, and several courtiers emerged from within the chamber. They were all dressed in clothing cut in the current fashion from the richest velvets and silks.

"What have we here?" The woman looked down her long nose, then glanced at her three companions. "Peasants roaming about the halls unescorted?"

Mikel drew himself to his full height, still not a match for her. "My blood is as blue as thine, Sophia."

"Oh, Mikel, it *is* thou." She offered him a fake smile. "I did not recognize thou in such finery." Her voice dripped with false sweetness.

Mikel did not flinch. "I don't waste my time on fancy clothing—I am a man, not some would-be peacock."

Her green eyes narrowed. "Isn't it past time for thou to return to thy country estates?" she asked, still in that too-sweet voice. "Don't the sheep miss thee?"

"As much as the other vipers miss thee."

Her face paled.

Mikel pushed past her.

Franz gave her a civil nod. "My Lady, Sophia." He followed his friend through the doors.

"Thou wished an audience?" Carolinka kept her voice light and her expression calm, even as the crowd parted before the arrival of two roughly garbed adventurers. Her dark hair was bound up in an elaborate coil atop her head, and rubies glittered on her earlobes.

Mikel glared up at the richly gowned woman atop the dais, taking no notice of the red stone columns, which supported the vaulted ceiling, nor the looks, and soft mutterings of the various courtiers he passed by. "Thou didn't want me to leave." He did not bother to mask the irritation in his voice, despite the courtiers who filled the room.

She nodded regally at him from her throne. "There is trouble within my barony." The red velvet cushions covered the seat, while the arms and legs were richly gilded.

"There is always trouble somewhere. I had a journey arranged."

"Thy journey can wait, I have need of you."

"Thou have liege-men and soldiers." Mikel gestured. Green-coated Guardsmen stood against the walls of the hall. "The city is filled with would-be heroes who would flock to thy side should thou call for volunteers."

She shook her head. "I do not want untrained adventurers. I want you."

"I am not interested."

Franz smiled. He stood a step behind Mikel and kept his hands hanging loosely at his sides. He glanced around the room, noting that the expressions of the courtiers ran the gauntlet from vaguely amused to outright horrified.

"The people are worried." Carolinka stood up with a smooth motion, then descended from her throne and began to pace the floor of the hall. Her silver-trimmed gown swished about her legs as she moved. "People's dreams are disturbed by visions of a dark Mother."

"And what concern is that of mine? What can I do about that? I cannot fight dreams. Call thy priests. Or thy mages."

"Both have proven powerless. These dreams are occurring more often. More and more people speak of them."

"What can I do about that?" Mikel repeated.

"People are going missing, cousin."

"And I am going to the Western Islands...once I find my horse."

"Forget those accursed islands! There is a mystery here at home."

"Another good reason to travel abroad."

"Mikel, ordinary townsfolk are going missing!" Her voice cracked, and raw emotion was plain. "Ones who dream and speak of the Mother often vanish without a trace. This is not my doing and the priesthoods are silent. The numbers of the missing are growing. No one has yet found the bodies."

Mikel frowned. "People do not simply vanish."

"These ones have."

Franz nodded and finally spoke. "So I have heard. Rumours and whispers in the ale-houses."

Mikel twisted his head around to look at his friend.

"These are more than just alehouse gossip, Franz. Entire villages have vanished in the night...this cannot possibly be permitted to continue." Carolinka's eyes flashed.

"Of course not."

"Thou must investigate this for me." She lowered her voice as she drew near. "I trust thee above any other. Find out what thou can, and then return to me or send word. We will hunt down whomever is responsible and then my army will exact its due vengeance."

"Why me?"

"Because thou are the best adventurer in my barony." Her expression softened. "And because I trust thee above all others."

"And because thou hid my favourite horse."

She smiled. "That as well."

Mikel offered her a ragged bow. "It would appear that I shall have no choice but to do as thou would command, my Lady."

"I am glad that we agree on this matter." Carolinka turned back towards her throne. "I will have information brought for thee. All rumours and tales and stories that we have heard. I would not dream of sending thee off without proper preparation."

Mikel's knuckles tightened on the hilt of his sword.

* * *

"How can she be holding a banquet tonight?" Mikel demanded as he pulled on his newly shined boots.

"The envoy from Baron Blucher has arrived with all due ceremony." Franz shrugged, and then he adjusted the drape of his cloak. "She wants to make a good impression on him." His clothes were of a fine cloth, and he had splashed on a spiced scent.

"To avoid a war."

"If the barony is threatened from within, now is not the time to risk any invasion from our neighbours. Carolinka is acting wisely to distract him."

"A waste of time. We should have been the road to the coast two mornings ago."

"We can ride forth to the coast tomorrow if thou so wish." Franz knew that Mikel would not leave for the Western Islands now. *Not until he learns the truth of these disappearances. Too many have vanished within the city walls for him to abandon his cousin.* "Enjoy thyself tonight. One night of merriment will not kill you." Franz chuckled. "Whatever we will be riding forth to face, however, just might."

The grand hall was brightly lit, despite the setting of the sun. Shadows danced on the stone walls, cast by a thousand candles and by scores of torches.

Servants wove through the clumps of courtiers carrying platters of snacks and drinks.

"I feel like a fool in this garb."

"You look like a courtier." Franz chuckled. "It's a rare sight to see thou dressed as befits a man of your station."

"This tunic itches." Mikel tugged at the collar to loosen it. The tunic was a bright green, with stripes of red woven through it. "The embroidery is all wrong."

"My mother sewed that for thee."

Mikel snatched a goblet from a passing servant. "He's even got his own banners flying." He hooked a thumb towards one of them hanging from the rafters.

"Sword transfixing a wolf's head. I wonder if that's symbolic?"

"Maybe the Baron's grandfather was a werewolf."

"It would not surprise me in the least, from what tales I have heard."

The envoy was dressed in rich cloth, with wolf fur trimming his cloak. Oliver Blucher surveyed the gathering with a penetrating gaze. He wore a black beard that he had trimmed into a sharp point and his eyes were cold.

Carolinka wore a pale red gown, with a low-cut neckline. She replaced the rubies in her ears with emeralds, and other green stones glittered on her fingers. She was slowly making her way through the room, pausing to chat with one group of nobles, before moving to another group where she again paused to talk.

"She seems to be enjoying herself."

Mikel snorted.

"Thou go up and introduce thyself to him."

"Hardly."

"The envoy might be a kindred soul."

"Shut up."

"Then I shall leave you, so that I might enjoy this evening." Franz reached for a goblet of wine from a tray which a serving girl was carrying past. "There is fine music and many fine ladies present. Good evening to thee."

Mikel watched his friend vanish into the crowd. "Damn."

Someone approached.

"Thou look like a man lost deep in thought," a resonant voice commented suddenly. "Though surely this is not the place for such deep thinking."

"Thy pardon, Baronet." Mikel blinked and tried to sound less bored. "I did not hear thee approach." He kept his left hand loosely gripped on the hilt of his sheathed sword.

"There is noise enough to drown a battle." Baronet Blucher offered the other man a smile. "Ye look like a man who has fought on many such fields." There was no warmth in that smile.

"Aye, as do thee." The Baronet stood with a dangerous grace, and Mikel noted that the hilt of his sword appeared to have been worn smooth from much use.

"So what was the nature of thy thoughts, ere I interrupted?"

"I was just wondering if this hall or the throne room was the larger."

The Baronet stroked his pointed beard with his left hand. "A good question." He looked around the grand hall with a measuring gaze. "I would guess that the throne room is larger. Though not by much."

Carolinka had paused near one fluted column, speaking with one of her ministers.

Oliver Blucher frowned slightly. "Are thee a member of this court?"

"Aye, in a manner of speaking."

"I did not see thee during my initial welcome." His frown deepened.

"I was not there." Mikel had been in the library. "My cousin failed to tell me the exact time of your arrival." *No doubt afraid that I would spill thy blood in a duel or some such.*

"Ah, her cousin. That explains much."

Explains what? Mikel wondered. "A distant cousin."

Servants paused as they wove their paths through the crowds, with platters of delicacies and trays of drinks held ready.

"Thy cousin has fine taste." The Baronet held up a crystal goblet and admired the way the warm candlelight glinted from its facets.

Carolinka was passing by, with several courtiers in tow.

"Ah, Baroness Grelfhaven."

She paused. "Baronet Blucher."

"My compliments on a fine reception."

"It is but a small token of welcome."

Blucher smiled—a trace more warmly than he had smiled at Mikel. "It is a most pleasant surprise. I did not know what welcome I should expect...given the rumours."

"Rumours?" Carolinka's voice was as bland as her expression.

"Yes, there is some talk of civil unrest in thy barony."

"There is no unrest," she replied calmly. "You must be listening to idle tavern gossip."

His eyes narrowed. "Then I have been misinformed?"

"Quite." Carolinka maintained her calm smile.

Mikel watched the interaction with a frown.

Baronet Blucher finished his wine and a servant hurriedly took the empty goblet from his hand. "I have heard rumours of disappearances."

"One must learn to separate truth from lies."

"Indeed. And thou?" he asked, turning to Mikel. "What do thou call 'truth' in these troubled times?"

"I try to avoid listening to alehouse gossip," he replied bluntly.

Oliver frowned and narrowed his grey eyes. His hand drifted towards his sword, but he did not grasp it.

"I believe," Mikel continued in a calm tone, "that should there prove to be some truth in any such wild rumours, then the Guards will be striving to find the miscreants and bring them to justice."

"A fine goal." The Baronet smoothed out his expression. "May it indeed be so."

Franz approached the small gathering. "A fine party, Baroness," he said, giving his cloak a flourish.

Carolinka gave him a smile.

· Chapter Four

"This morning came too damned early." Franz squinted against the sun, which had crested the parapet and was spilling down into the stable yard.

Mikel was checking the saddle straps on his horse. "Thou chose to stay overlong at the reception. I knew enough to leave and seek out my bed."

"Aye, thou were wiser than I. However, I got to know some of the envoy's party."

"I saw thou eying that girl."

"She was the envoy's wife. We just talked."

"Sure thou did."

"Of course we just talked." Franz grunted and bent down to pick his saddlebags from the ground. "Then I chatted with one of the Baronet's men-at-arms. Swordmaster Johannes and I discussed the art of the sword for quite some time. Three or four goblets of wine it took. I think we both might have fought in one of the border skirmishes ten winters back or so. I don't recall facing him blade-to-blade, but it's certainly possible."

Mikel silently shook his head.

Franz finished tying his saddlebags on. "So what is thy plan?"

"We ride north." Mikel climbed into his saddle. "Beaudral is the closest village. The Court has received word that people there are dreaming of a Dark Mother. Carolinka said that such dreams seem to forewarn of disappearances."

"I thought the dark dreams were coming from within the city?"

"Thy friendly priest claims that his order will seek out the corruption within our walls." Mikel chuckled. "He made quite the fiery speech to the court, all but promising fire and brimstone to come raining down from the heavens at his call."

"Josem is less than a friend to me. An acquaintance really."

"Oh? Do you two go drinking and carousing?"

Franz grunted.

"Am I missing out on some fine alehouse gossip by not going with the pair of thee?"

"Josem is hardly the sort to frequent an alehouse." Franz gestured. "Let the priests watch the city. Leave the wilderness to us then."

"Aye."

"So we two adventurers are set to ride to stop some invisible army?"

"I ride forth to investigate. If thou choose to accompany me...."

Franz chuckled. "Like I would trust thou to travel far without me to guard thy back." He mounted his own horse. "A pleasant day for a ride."

"More pleasant if *I* was riding to the sea."

"Why venture forth on a ship? What adventure can there be among the ruins that ye could not find here?"

"The ruins are more likely to be filled with unclaimed treasure than the northern forests."

"Mayhap you speak truth, but the one never knows just what adventure or treasure can be found."

"Let's ride. Sunlight is wasting." Mikel flicked his reins.

One of the seven guardsmen at the inner gate nodded as the two equestrians approached. "Off for a ride, my Lords?" He eyed their bulging saddlebags and swords. None of the other guardsmen said a word.

"Aye, Devon." Franz nodded.

"A fine day for it." The Guardsman nodded and then leaned more heavily on his spear. "Take a gallop to clear the last of the wine fumes from one's head."

"The morning air *is* crisp and sharp," Mikel agreed. The wind was tugging at his cloak. "Good morning to ye." He gave the reins a flick.

"A most pleasant morning for a ride," Franz agreed as the two rode slowly along a gravel path, through a courtyard dominated by a fountain. "Just who is that supposed to be?"

Mikel glanced at the statue they were riding past. "I have gazed upon its likeness a thousand times and I have no idea," he admitted.

"She is some ancestor of thine, is she not?"

"I don't know. She could be the first Baroness. She could be the mistress of some noble or the imagination of some nameless sculptor." Her face was one of nondescript serenity, smiling. Water issued from openings in her neck to cascade over her limbs like some phantom gown. "It matters not. Come on."

Franz chuckled.

* * *

The two horsemen made good time as they rode along the tree-lined main streets of the capitol. The early-morning crowds were thin, and they parted easily before the horsemen.

With a loud crunch, Franz bit into a green apple he had bought from a hawker. "Speaking again of my priest, I saw Josem in the marketplace two days past."

"Was it his turn to preach?" Mikel slowed as a trio of Dwarfs hurried across the street in front of them. The three were arguing loudly in their own tongue.

"No," Franz continued, "he was shopping. Or browsing. Or whatever it is that priests do in the marketplace. Surely they must purchase goods and chattels like the rest of us. Anyway, I saw this one hawker who claimed to have a tame dragon on display."

"Did he?"

"I did not pay the coins to find out." Franz shrugged. "I have seen dragons before and without paying good silver to do so. Recall the Wyrm of Black Fen Swamp? Now there was a fearsome beast. Thirty paces from the tip of its snout to the last barb on its tail. Thirty paces at least and—"

"You were talking about the priest?"

"Oh, aye. I had just left the hawker when Josem hailed me. We spoke a moment of idle news, and then I saw and listened to a man raving about some new fertility cult."

"The Mother?"

"Aye."

Mikel frowned. "I've heard of it a few times now. Even before Carolinka summoned us. Heard stories and rumours around the palace, I mean. Usually a retelling of some overheard ravings by some wild-eyed lunatic. Note that the teller was less of a lunatic."

Franz took another bite of his apple. "There was nearly a riot this time. Took a full squad of the City Guards to break it up and escort the preacher to the cells. Josem got off with a warning and a fine."

"A fine?"

"For 'disturbing the peace'. He was not pleased."

"I can't imagine that he would be."

"So the cult spreads within the city and countryside alike."

"Aye, if it is just a cult."

Franz narrowed his eyes. "And if it is not?" he asked. He tossed his apple core into the gutter.

A woman wearing a bright blue bonnet glared at him for a moment, then hurried on her way.

"Then what would it be?" Mikel waved aside a man selling meat pies. "The finest beef thou claim? More likely cat."

"Never, my Lord." The man looked offended, but he hurried vanished into the crowd before Mikel could say more.

"Fertility cults often attract large crowds at the start. Consider the nature of their worship and ritual?" Franz chuckled a moment, before he sobered. "If this is not simply the normal rise of some new religious cult, then what might it be? Some foul plot to undermine the barony?"

"Carolinka won't be caught short by some plot."

"No, but the city could be gripped by real riots. Fertility cults or not, things could become violent."

"We'll find out the truth soon enough. I swore to solve the mystery and I will keep my word."

The city gates came into view at long last. A dozen men-at-arms stood guard, watching the flow of traffic passing through the open gates. They all carried spears and shields emblazoned with the stylized oak tree that symbolized the Baroness's family line. Their green cloaks flapped in the wind.

"A fertility cult...and dreams of a Dark Mother."

"Thou believe there is some connection?"

"I do." Mikel directed his horse around a stopped wagon.

Once through the gates, the crowds thinned out completely.

Mikel reined in his mount.

"There's no one on the roads." Franz could count the number of wagons he saw on one hand.

"Well, 'tis early yet."

Several of the men-at-arms were watching them.

"And now for a decent gallop!" Mikel flicked the reins. "Come on!" His cloak billowed out behind him.

"Aye!" Franz gave chase.

· **Chapter Five**

Beaudral was a typical village.

"Small, boring. Nothing but sheep and cows for leagues and leagues. Not a decent alehouse for even more leagues I dare wager."

"Thou could have stayed back in the capitol."

"True, but of late it's even more boring there." Franz eyed the streets. Hard-packed dirt, rutted by the wheels of countess wagons, ran between the single-story buildings. "No guards."

"This is a small village. Why would they have guards?" Mikel loosened the ties of his shirt. "It's growing quite warm."

Franz kept the cowl of his cloak pulled up. "We should stop at the inn and arrange rooms for our stay." He could hear sounds of a blacksmith hard at work someplace near.

"And get some food. I am tired of flatbread and cheese."

"Travellers' rations are best. Thou have grown to used to the rich foods of the court."

"I have grown used to good food."

"A few weeks in the saddle will help work that off." Franz paused. "I could do with a drink though, to wash the dust of the road from my throat."

"An alehouse would have the latest news as well."

"Aye, 'tis truth that ye speak. But will we find an alehouse which serves decent vintages?"

"That will remain a mystery for a time." Mikel eyed the buildings.

* * *

Mikel could still taste the ale on his tongue as he stepped back into the street. *Bitter and poorly brewed stuff he served us. Little wonder the alehouse does little trade.* He adjusted his sword-belt.

Franz spat into the dirt. "Gah," he muttered. "That swill was more vinegar than wine. To think that he thought we would take rooms here. I have no desire to sleep amid filth and vermin. I'd rather sleep under a bush, or in some hayloft."

There were some people walking through the streets.

"They look scared." Mikel wore his dark blue cloak draped loosely over his shoulders, keeping enough free movement so that he could easily grab his sword from where it rode at his waist if the need arose.

"Thou heard the innkeeper." Franz nodded to passing villagers...and took note of the frightened stares he received in return. "Twenty people have vanished so far. Travellers on the road. Farmers from the more isolated farmsteads. Townsfolk abroad late at night. That's enough to frighten anyone."

"Aye, but *who* is responsible."

"That *is* the burning question."

"No one is moving about alone." Mikel hooked his thumb at one cluster of men standing near the blacksmith's forge. "Everyone is sticking together in groups."

"Do thou blame them?" Franz eyed them, then abruptly dismissed them as a threat. "I doubt those pitchforks they carry will aid them in much should an attack come." Untrained farmers would be more likely to injure themselves should an enemy attack them.

"They will use what they can. They're not trained warriors."

"Why should they be?" Franz rested his hand on the hilt of his sword. The feel of the place was making him uneasy. "They have the armies of the Baroness to protect their lands from raiders and bandits." He paused, silently acknowledging that the current raiders were apparently more than the routine patrols could handle.

Mikel stepped around a muddy puddle. "From what tales we were told, people vanish almost exclusively at night."

"Aye, but how much longer will they trust the sun with people continue to vanish? What stops this foe from preying on them by daylight?"

"Some spell? Some trait that limits them to night's cloaking shadow?"

"Possibly. A pity we could not find a mage willing to accompany us."

"What need have we of mages? In all our many adventures, how often have we fought against mages? I trust in the strength of my sword far more than in some muttered spell."

"If we face a foe who wields the arcane arts, then we shall see how effective thy sword truly is."

"No mage has yet been born who can cast a spell once good steel has been driven through his heart."

"Assuming we can venture close enough to plunge the steel home."

"The world would be a better place without sorcery."

"That is thy opinion."

"Aye, it is."

"We two might be overly pressed by the foe. If there is not simply one murderer loose in the night...."

"Then we will need allies."

"Once we find the truth of this mystery, we'll have mages and armies to march with us." A sudden gust of wind tugged at his cloak and Franz shivered at its strange chill. "Time enough for more talk in the tavern later."

"Aye, time enough." Mikel eyed the street again. No one was meeting his eye. *No children are running in the streets. Few women. This place has the stench of fear.* "Back to the tavern then?"

"I suppose."

"It will be a sleepless night for us, of that I have little doubt. Better to rest now and be fresh for the darkness."

Franz nodded. "Aye, let us return to the inn then. A few hours in flea-infested blankets will still be restful."

"But I will not eat more of that stew." Mikel shook his head. "That first bowl was simply foul."

"We're just travellers, not regulars, so why should we expect something grand?" Franz paused to examine a display of fruit placed on a small table outside one of the shops. *Those withered apples look like they were harvested ten years ago.* He looked at the shopkeeper.

The man did not meet his eyes.

"I expect something edible," Mikel complained. "That stew tasted like boiled boots."

"Now that ye mention it, it did bear more than a passing resemblance to the stews served by the Army cooks while we were last on campaign." Franz frowned. "Have ye any fresher apples?"

"Nay, good master." The shopkeeper shook his head. "The wagons are late in coming."

Franz tossed him a coin. "Then this shall have to do." He took a relatively large red apple and bit into it. "Not too bitter. The inn should be used to travellers...we are not that far from the capitol." *Two days, or so, by horse....* He took another bite. "Yet this has proven to be a lightly travelled road. How many other riders have we passed by? Two wagons? Three?"

"Who was counting," Mikel countered. "Five, maybe six."

"We should have seen more than that in a single day, let alone in two. People are not travelling along this road."

"There are other villages. It's not harvest season yet."

"Still, there should be traffic."

"If there was no traffic, then the merchants in the city would have been complaining. I heard no such complaints at court."

"Nor did I. And I frequent places more likely to hear such tales."

"So what is the reason?"

"I have none as yet." Franz took another bite of his apple. "But it worries me."

* * *

"Night is approaching."

"And everyone is scurrying for shelter." Mikel looked around, but the village streets were already all but deserted.

"It looks like many of the people who are out are headed for the temple."

"More of them headed to the tavern." Mikel frowned and patted the hilt of his sword. "I could use a mug of ale to wet my throat."

"Time enough for drinking after we have checked the village." Franz had drawn his sword and now he gave it a practice swing. "Thou heard the alehouse talk. These things come in the night."

"What things? It could just be brigands."

Franz snorted. "Do thou truly think this is the work of brigands?" he asked. "Twenty people vanishing? No plundering or looting? Men and women and children simple gone missing ere morning's light."

"Nay," Mikel admitted, "'tis not the work of normal bandits."

Franz nodded. "We must work cautiously. There is danger here."

"At least the sky is clear. We'll have a moon to see by."

"For all the good that will do us."

"Aye."

A night bird called out. An owl hooted.

"The attacks are far too efficient and deadly to be the work of bandits. Brigands would leave some trace, some sign to mark their presence." Mikel adjusted his cloak.

"From rumour, there is no such mark. There is no mark."

"I know."

They paced along the street, their boots crunching softly in the dirt.

"What do thou think of the other travellers?"

"Thou saw them?"

Franz nodded.

"Adventurers. Possibly one step up from brigands themselves." Mikel shook his head at the memory of the wild boasting that trio had made over their ale. "Not much help in a battle, and more likely hindrance." *Especially given the amount of ale they drank. They'll be lucky to remain awake, let alone standing for any length of time.* "They be passed out in a heap ere long."

"My thoughts as well. They were headed south."

"Then we shall patrol northward. Close to the forest."

"I thought much the same."

"The innkeeper seemed pleased by our offer to patrol this night."

"He still made us pay for our beds in advance," Mikel pointed out.

"He likely wants his coin in case we should be slain in the night."

"Such confidence."

Franz shrugged. "Beaudral has lost many so far." He kept turning his head, scanning the village.

"Farmers, not warriors."

"Should there be many foe to outnumber us, we also might fall. Trained warriors or not."

"I doubt that. Thou are too skilled with a blade to fall easily."

"Flatterer. Come, let us walk this way." Franz turned into a narrow street. *More alley than street,* he thought.

"Did ye see something?"

"Nay, just listening to a hunch. Something ye should learn to do more often."

Mikel nodded, his eyes jumping from shadow to shadow. "Aye, so ye tell me often enough."

Chapter Six

"Night darkened hovels and muddy streets. We really need to travel to better places."

Mikel chuckled. "Aye, that we do." He stepped around a foul-smelling puddle. "The streets are too quiet."

"Not even a dog. We should hear at least one dog barking, right?"

"Would that we might be back in the capitol with torches to light the streets." At least the important streets were lit thusly. "There be no lamplighters' guild out here."

"Not as yet. Mayhap ye should retire and start a chapter."

"Too many people go to sleep as the sun does." Such was the life of poor farmers, or so Mikel reckoned it.

The moon emerged from behind a cloud.

Shadows moved across the street.

"What's that?"

"Brigands?" Franz reached for his sword and drew it slowly from its sheath. "Or our erstwhile allies?"

One of the moving shadows resolved into a cow-like shape with a wildly elongated head.

"By the Gods!"

The creature parted its jaws and hissed. Double sets of jaws opened, revealing razor-like fangs. It was covered in a dully-gleaming greenish-blue carapace.

"What is it?" Franz demanded. "Some kind of deformed Minotaur?"

"An insect more-like." Mikel raised his own sword. "Come on then, monster!" He saw no eyes on the beast's head, but it had two rows of stubby horns.

Franz gave his sword a practice swing.

A man with a scraggly red beard stepped around the corner of a dark building. He wore a ragged brown cloak over his bronze robes. "I thought as much." He hurried forward, raising his white ash staff.

Mikel saw him come. "No, get away!"

The monster hissed again and reared up on its hind legs, standing like a man. Its long tail lashed back and forth and it flexed its claw-tipped hands.

"I banish thee back into the Infernal Pits from whence thou spawned!" The man gestured with his staff.

"Get back, fool!" Mikel shouted.

Lightning flashed from the end of the staff and blasted the creature.

Mikel and Franz cried out as their eyes were blinded.

A piercing shriek rang out and a terrible stench filled the air.

Franz coughed and blinked his eyes repeatedly. "Ye Gods...'tis like a burning middenheap."

Mikel kept a tight grip on his sword.

Silence, and darkness, descended back onto the street. Neither closed doors nor shuttered windows opened.

"It is slain." The bearded man slumped, leaning heavily on his staff for support. "Ye Gods."

Mikel eyed the other man. "Can thou explain what that was?" He did not sheath his sword.

The man shook his head. "Not easily."

"Will there be more of them lurking around?" Franz asked. "Or do such beasts hunt alone?"

"This one is alone. The village is safe enough now."

"And the farms?"

"I cannot speak for them. Beaudral is safe enough." The man straightened. "I would sense them if others were near."

Franz grunted. "I need a drink."

"Thou are a mage then, Geoff?"

Geoff nodded. "Aye." He took a drink of what was claimed to be the alehouse's best wine and grimaced. "Damned small villages. 'Tis impossible to get a decent drink. Still, what choice is there?" He took another drink and then looked across the table. "Aye, gentlemen, I have some training in the mystical arts."

"That is no fit beard for a mage." Mikel sounded scornful. He spat into the sawdust which covered the floor. "Every mage I have seen has a long flowing beard."

"And have thou seen many mages, *traveller*?"

Mikel nodded at the mage's mocking tone. "Enough of them." Many men, and some few women, flocked to the Court often enough, seeking audiences with the Baroness. "Thou have the clothes and staff, but not the bearing."

"Nor the beard," Franz added.

"I am not a Dwarf."

"That much is obvious."

"I am Geoff." He patted at his somewhat worn bronze robes and looked around the tavern. "Thou are lucky that I happened along. Thy swords would have proved no match for that beast."

"Beast? Thou would claim that thing was a wild beast?"

"I am inclined to agree with Franz. That was a demon straight from the deepest pit of the Inferno."

Silently, Geoff took another drink.

"Do thou disagree with him?"

Geoff offered them a shrug. "The evidence does point towards a less than mundane origin for those creatures, though I fear thou jump to wild conclusions."

"So then what was it?" Mikel swallowed a draught from his own mug. The tavern was crowded, as if no one wanted to be alone. Men were drinking and talking furtively. Women sat at the tables as well, with their children. So far, no one took overmuch notice of the trio.

The handful that did, looked away as soon as any of the trio glanced back at them.

Geoff frowned. "It was...akin to dragon kind."

"That was a dragon?" Franz allowed cold scorn to fill his voice. "Don't be daft, man. I fought a dragon near the Ash Hills and that beast was nothing like this one. There were no sweeping wings, no blasts of flame. So was the Wyrm of the Black Fens."

"'Twas very undragon-like," Mikel agreed.

"It lacked proper scales. Our beast was shining like some monstrous beetle."

Mikel turned his attention back to Geoff. "Was it dragon, demon, or insect then?"

"I am not sure...but I like this not. Thou interfered with my work."

"We were sent by the Baroness to investigate travellers' tales about missing villagers and things spurring unrest."

"Then thou can return to her with reports of the beast's death. Thy problem is solved."

Mikel grunted. "Thou slew it with magic."

"Aye."

"Would my blade have proven deadly to it as well? Answer me," he pressed. "Unless ye have something to hide."

"Aye..." the mage nodded with some reluctance. "Assuming that thou lived long enough to use it. These Chthonians are not to be tackled easily. They are far more deadly than any beast thou might have encountered or indeed ever heard of."

"It looked vaguely like a Minotaur."

"Aye, it did bear some traces of such ancestry."

"A demon-dragon is not something I'd wish to face often," Mikel said and reached for his clay mug. "Are there more of them around?"

Geoff nodded reluctantly. "Probably."

A black-bearded Dwarf swaggered over to their table and took a seat uninvited. He leaned his axe against the tavern wall, then stared across the time-worn table at them. "Talking about them new dragons are ye?"

Geoff flinched. "Thou have seen them?"

"Aye. Norvgan is the name. Norvgan Ironbeard." He took a drink from the mug he had been carrying, and then slammed it down onto the table.

People at other tables jumped at the noise.

"Five of those damnable beasts attacked my convoy not a quarter moon past. They killed three of my companions, and carried off two others. I tracked the lot of them here to Beaudral."

Mikel's brown eyes narrowed. "They lair within this village?"

Norvgan shrugged. "I lost the trail nearby, but I plan to track them down. They owe me a blood price."

"They cannot be laired within the village...surely they would have been spotted by the villagers."

"They do not lair here," Geoff informed them in a confident tone. "I would know." He leaned back in his chair.

"I tracked five of them into the forest near here," Norvgan insisted. "Do ye doubt my word?"

"Of course not." The mage shook his head. "But I know what I know."

"There are many ruined farmsteads in the woods." Franz gestured northward. "They were sacked and pillaged during the Goblin raids some three winters back. Most of them were never resettled."

"A good place for us to begin looking then."

"I'm with ye. I owe them things a blood-debt." Norvgan reached for the carved handle of his axe.

"I do not know about this."

"Peace, Geoff. I have fought alongside Dwarfs before...his axe will be of much help to us."

Geoff glared at Mikel. "Perhaps I do not wish to have *thy* assistance in this task."

Mikel glared back. "Perhaps *thou* have no choice."

The mage straightened his back and assumed a haughty air, which looked out of place given his youthful face. "Thou are seeking to meddle with things not of this world. I cannot promise to be able to protect thee."

"We don't need thy protection. We'll do fine on our own."

Geoff said nothing, though his face was pale.

Norvgan drained his mug. "More ale!" he shouted to the barmaid and everyone in the tavern jumped. "Tonight we drink...tomorrow, hopefully, we spill blood!"

Geoff's face grew paler.

Chapter Seven

The sun was halfway to its peak.

"I need more than just three hours of sleep," Franz muttered.

"Thou are getting old," Mikel teased. "Ye lack the vigour of youth when ye have a head full of cheap ale. 'Tis a fine time to be on a quest."

"Thou talk too much." Franz stopped. The trail curved through the forest and the undergrowth limited visibility to a just few yards.

Geoff frowned as he stepped over a fallen sapling. "I have never liked forests." His robes were just not practical for cross-country travelling.

"The farmsteads should be just ahead. I recall fighting here during the raids." Franz looked around, squinting into the underbrush. "Yep, there's the lightning struck oak. The bolt came down during one fierce swordfight. I thought the Gods themselves were taking sides that day."

"Seems awfully quiet for a forest."

"The battle was three winters back, Dwarf."

"I mean for now, Manling." Norvgan looked around with a scowl on his face. He was gripping his axe tightly. "Shouldn't there be birds chirping? Some furry things rustling about? Noise of all sorts?"

"The Dwarf is right." Geoff had stopped moving and he was looking around the forest. "It *is* too quiet." His hand was white-knuckled as he tightened the grip on his ash staff. "Far too quiet."

"Another of thy dragons?"

"Perhaps."

The leafy junipers rustled.

Geoff half-raised his staff.

A red-tailed squirrel dashed out of the junipers and climbed up into an oak where it perched on a branch and chattered at them.

"See," Geoff said in relief, "'tis just an animal."

The junipers rustled again and something squealed.

"Must be a large one this time," Norvgan commented.

The creature which lifted its elongated head out of the undergrowth was no squirrel. Its insect-like carapace glinted a dull greenish-blue in the sun. Bright red blood dripped from its double row of fangs. It looked even more nightmarish in the sunlight, now that it could clearly be seen.

"Dragon!" Norvgan hefted his axe.

"That's no dragon, ye daft fool." Franz had his sword drawn.

Mikel spat. "Then what is it?" He held his own blade ready, but was unwilling to charge blindly.

"'Tis one of *them*." The Dwarf took a firmer grip on his axe.

"Then it dies." Mikel gestured. "Franz, move to the left. We'll distract it with numbers. Norvgan, ye should—"

"I'll lop its head from its neck." The creature's neck did look absurdly thin to support such an overly large head. "And that be just the start." The Dwarf took a step forward.

The creature hissed at him.

The mage shook his head, his face pale behind his scraggly beard. "Stay away from it!" He raised his staff. "Run, fools!"

Mikel stood his ground.

"We need archers," Franz said as the creature hissed again. He was eying its claws carefully.

"Archers?" Mikel shook his head. "Against that?"

The dragon lunged forward, leaping through the bushes and scattering leaves and branches in the air behind it.

"I banish thee!" Geoff unleashed a blast from the tip of his staff.

"Gods of the Deep!" Norvgan scowled. "That thing smells like a Goblin warren after one of their holy festivals." He spat onto the ground.

With a grimace, Mikel sheathed his sword. "Thou slew another one, mage."

"Aye." Geoff eyed the charred corpse with distaste. He lowered his staff and leaned on it. He took several deep breaths, despite the stench.

"Convenient then that these beasts stalk their prey alone."

"Oh, the Chthonians hunt in groups as well." Geoff poked at the corpse with his staff and it crumbled into grey ash. "They will come in force soon enough. Once they breed their numbers large enough."

"As well that we have thee then, Mage, with thy ability to summon forth such potent bolts of lightning."

Mikel shook his head, then stepped away from Franz. "Why do thou call them *Chthonians*? Aren't they dragons?"

"Or demon-dragons?"

Geoff glanced at the Dwarf. "They are a beast all but unknown on this world. In one of the old tongues, *Chthonian* refers to things of a *hellish* nature. These things are truly demons spawned from the pits of Hell so it seems quite appropriate to name them thusly."

Franz whistled. "The old tongue, eh?"

"The Nostronomun tongue."

Geoff's eyes darted towards the Dwarf.

Norvgan smiled calmly. "Dwarfs have long memories."

Geoff scowled. "They do indeed." There was little sound of admiration in his voice, but rather substantial disgruntlement.

"It has been a hundred generations for you Manlings, but a merely a quarter of that for my kin."

"So these creatures are named after the Nostronomun demons?" Mikel shook his head at such a thought. "Those were just myths." The wind tugged at his cloak, but he ignored it.

"Myths often have a basis in fact."

"As ye say."

"Events are told stories, which in turn become myth." Geoff cleared his throat. "Myth turns to legend and legend is eventually forgotten." He did not mask the sadness or regret in his voice. "No library endures forever. Knowledge lost is difficult to recover."

"But not impossible."

"Everything ages and fades," Norvgan commented. "Even the mountains are eventually washed away by the rains." He looked at the mage. "Even magic fades."

"I do not argue that," Geoff countered. "Even the mightiest wielder of the arcane arts knows nothing more of *Milking Tears* or *Riding With The Sun* that the names of the forgotten spells."

"This is all interesting," Franz interjected, "but a forest clearing hardly seems the place to talk about myths. Shouldn't we continue the hunt?"

"Or have we slain all of these Chthonians?"

Geoff flinched at the accusation in Mikel's tone. "There will be more." He began walking along the overgrown path.

"How many more of these demons are we likely to face?" Norvgan demanded as he followed.

"I am not certain." Geoff did not look happy admitting his ignorance. He held his staff loosely in his hand. "These are mysterious creatures...there are no simple answers when thou face them.

"Do thou think we got them all?" Mikel asked after several minutes of silence. He turned his head to look at the Dwarf who was tramping along in the party's rear. "Thou claimed to have fought *five* of these beasts?"

Norvgan nodded. "Aye."

"There's the stream, just like I remember. The farmhouse should be just ahead." Franz gestured. "How many did thou slay, Norvgan?"

The Dwarf glared at Franz.

The Human stared back. "Well?"

"None!" Norvgan spat on the ground. "None. Damn ye for asking! I was knocked unconscious during the first charge and rolled beneath our wagon. I awoke to find my companions dead or vanished. There were no bodies to show if they slew any of these creatures ere they perished."

"I have struck down five of the beasts." Geoff carefully eyed the ruined farmhouse as it finally came into view. It was half-burned, and partially collapsed on itself. "Two of them in thy company—one in the village and another just now—and three others on my own journeying. I would hope that we have slain them all." He polished the end of his staff nervously with his sleeve. "I devoutly hope so."

Norvgan grimaced. "We need to go inside."

"After thou then."

Mikel had his sword drawn and held tightly in his grip. "We all go." There was no arguing with his tone.

The yard was overgrown with weeds.

"It seems too quiet." Geoff looked around and scratched his head. "Shouldn't there be feral chickens running around or something?"

"Aye, there should be." Mikel nodded. "Something must have eaten them."

Geoff paled.

"The barn is over there."

"It's a wreck. That would be no shelter from anything." Norvgan looked around and sniffed at the air. "'Tis too open for my taste in this place."

Geoff wandered closer. "We must search everywhere. If we overlook a potential hiding spot, we risk our lives. These creatures could be breeding almost anywhere." He maintained an easy grip on his staff.

"The mage is right." Franz gestured with his sword. "Keep thy eyes open. We can trust nothing in this place."

Norvgan kept a firm grip on his axe. "I never trust anything above ground. The surface world is too open and far too bright."

Geoff shook his head. "Children. I am surrounded by children." He poked his staff under a fallen rafter.

Mikel peered inside the remains of the barn. "I don't see anything nesting in here."

"Keep looking." Geoff paused. "I can sense something ill in the aura of this place."

"Can thou be more specific?"

"No."

Something hissed at them.

"I banish you!"

When the crackle of lightning had faded, Mikel coughed on the smoke that lingered. "What is it with thou and lightning?" he asked loudly.

Geoff shrugged, then adjusted his brown cloak as a cold wind gusted through the yard. "I like lightning," he replied.

"Why not cast a fireball? Or a freezing wind?"

Geoff gripped his ash staff. "I like lightning," he repeated. "Just be thankful that I can cast something that can slay these demons."

"I still need to slay one of these damnable demons," Norvgan snarled. He gave his axe a swing. "At least one must fall to my axe."

Franz eyed him. "We have found one...there might yet be more."

"I know."

"Then we should check the farmhouse."

"Aye."

"With caution." Geoff grimaced and shook his head. "The aura is...."

"Yes, the aura is disturbed." Mikel hefted his sword. "Let's go."

Norvgan pushed open the farmhouse door. "'Tis empty."

"For now." Geoff stepped inside.

Sunlight shining through cracks in the walls and missing thatch on the roof showed an all-but-empty room. There was little intact furniture in the room, but much that spoke of violence. A table that had been hacked into pieces; broken pottery on the floor; torn clothing scattered like useless rags.

"No sign of life."

"No signs of un-life either." Geoff looked around, then he closed his eyes and inhaled deeply, despite the dust hanging in the air. "I feel a presence. There is a dark aura to this place."

"The cellar?" Norvgan gestured to a trapdoor in the floor. "There is always a cellar in these farmhouses."

Mikel and Franz grasped the handle and hefted the door open.

Rickety-looking stairs led into darkness.

"It smells."

Mikel wrinkled his nose. "The Dwarf is right. It smells like there be a marsh down there." The air rising past his face was humid.

"After you then," Franz said with a wave.

Mikel grinned. "After the Dwarf."

"I have no qualms about venturing beneath the ground." Norvgan hefted his axe. "Put me in my proper element and ye will see a true warrior."

Geoff pushed past and peered down into the cellar. "Stay back!" he cried, his voice mingling horror and fear.

"What?"

"Stay back." Geoff had gone pale, his eyes wide. "Ye Gods," he swore. "Ye blessed Gods." He gripped his staff more tightly. "None of thou must venture below...the cellar contains sights too terrible for thy minds to accept. Thou would lose thy tenuous grasp on sanity and be driven insane."

Franz frowned.

"But—"

"Do not argue, Mikel. I am a mage...we are protected from such things." He took a deep breath. "I hope." He stepped onto the first step, then closed his eyes a moment. "Watch and allow nothing to flee from this place."

"Nothing?"

"Nothing."

"What sort of *nothing* should we be watching for?"

Geoff did not answer the Dwarf, but took another step into the cellar.

The crackle of lightning erupted from under the floor.

Mikel looked at Franz. "Should we go and help?" He took a step forward, towards the trap door.

"He told us to remain here." Franz looked calm even as more lightning crackled and the house trembled. He did have his sword drawn though.

Something shrieked.

Norvgan spat on the floor. "Just like a snotty mage. Take off on ye and steal all the treasure."

"What treasure?"

"They're dragons, ain't they? However odd they look...they must have a hoard."

Smoke was billowing through the trapdoor and the men recoiled at the stench.

"Ye Gods," Mikel coughed. "Ye Gods."

Geoff stumbled up the stairs. "I have cleansed this place of its nest," he said, "but I am weak." His robes were tattered and stained with greenish ichors and unnameable fluids and his cloak was missing. "We must leave here and never return." The smoke was growing thicker and reddish light flickered at his feet. "The cleansing flames will purify this place."

Geoff staggered into the stream and flung himself into the waters.

Franz watched, then looked away. "The farmhouse is burning."

"As well it should. That place is cursed." Geoff splashed water into his face. "Cursed." There was a tone of madness in his voice. "We are all cursed." Water dripped through his beard.

Mikel waded into the stream. "Geoff."

The mage stared at him with haunted eyes.

"What did thou see?"

"Sights no mortal should ever see." Geoff staggered back onto the shore and collapsed in the grass. "I can only pray that we have slain all those demons. Should any remain—even a single beast—they will breed more of their foul kind and disaster will be loosed upon the world."

Norvgan grunted.

Chapter Eight

"The village is quiet."

"This place is not." Norvgan looked around the busy tavern. "It finally seems to be coming to life." He reached for his mug of ale.

"Ye cannot blame the villagers for laying low. With the threat of death stalking them by night, what would you expect?"

"A Dwarf hold would have sent out hunters, not cowered in their beds by night."

"These are men, not Dwarfs."

"Do not men dream of glory and adventure?"

"Not all men. Some dream happily of wives and children." Mikel gestured to the crowded tavern. "Like these." Almost every table was filled with people talking and drinking. Unlike the previous evening, these people were boisterous and loud, singing and toasting their good fortune. *They drink and celebrate in the streets as well. No one is unhappy on this night.* He glanced at one table. *Well, perhaps the adventurers are dismayed by the way, things turned out.* He was surprised to see that the trio had survived; they were seated at one table, staring sourly into their mugs. "Some people dream of glory, others have glory forced upon them."

Geoff finally spoke up. "And sometimes 'tis just nightmares."

"Regular nightmares you mean." Mikel glanced at Geoff. The mage had spoken but rarely in the last two days. "The village of Beaudral is at peace. I have sent word back to the capitol by messenger."

"Carolinka will be pleased then. She wanted the attacks ended."

"And ended they are," Geoff agreed. "For now."

Franz eyed him. "Do ye know something different? Or are thou just a gloomy type by nature?"

Geoff tugged at the collar of his robe. "Ye would be happy and hope that we have won? That we have slain all of the dragons?"

"Until I see proof otherwise, yes." Franz drank deeply from his mug. "Why worry otherwise?"

"The ale tastes better," Norvgan said as he drained his mug.

"It could probably be worse."

"Ye Manlings cannot seem to master the art of brewing a decent ale. Ye should send apprentices to the halls of my kin and learn the arts properly."

A young tavern serving girl set fresh clay mugs onto the table. "My Lords?" She wore a low-cut green blouse, with her red skirts slashed up to her thighs. "Another round for thee?"

"Thou has my thanks," Norvgan told her.

She gave the Dwarf a smile, but turned up its intensity as she looked at Mikel and Franz. "If there is anything ye should wish, then ye need only ask."

Mikel smiled at her, noting just how low-cut her blouse was. "We are fine. Thanks for the ale."

"Kathe, my Lords." She gave them another curtsey. "The whole village knows that thou have saved us from the Chthonians." She stumbled over the unusual word. "We are in thy debt."

"It is the duty of the strong to defend the weak." Franz finished draining his first mug and reached for a second. "'Twas but our duty." He half stood, so that he could offer her a half-bow.

"It was vengeance." Norvgan grimaced and reached for his mug. "They owed a blood-price. They owe it still," he added grimly.

"It was our duty," Mikel agreed. He offered a smile to her. "And worth doing to know that it has raised a shadow from thy face. Now thou can rest and dream peacefully."

Her blush deepened. "Some of us have dreamed. Oh, not since thou slew all the demons and burned their nest, but before. We—they—I—dreamed of a tower."

"A tower?" Geoff sounded startled.

"Aye, standing near the river, with mountains rising in the west."

"What kind of mountains?"

Kathe frowned. "Black jagged ones, with fog and cloud wreathing their peaks."

"And the tower?"

"Squat and thick, built of grey stone. Twas but a dream, my Lords."

"Sounds like one of the Barony's watch towers, near the Shadow Peaks," the Dwarf commented as he looked across the table.

Mikel glanced across the table at Franz. "Thou served near the Peaks."

"Aye, fighting off Goblin raids." He sipped calmly at his mug. "It does sound like one of the Stone Watchers."

"Perhaps we should venture there next."

"Aye."

"A dream ye say?" Geoff looked at her intently. "What else did thou dream?"

The maiden flushed. "Oh, nothing, my Lord Mage."

"Speak," Geoff persisted. "Tell me everything." He leaned forward and reached for her wrist, catching it in his hand. "Speak of thy dream," he ordered in a low tone.

"I—I dreamed that my mother was there." She shrugged and attempted to laugh. "Foolishness it is. That's what my Da called it. Foolishness."

"Thy mother was in the tower? Calling to thee?"

"My mother died in the Snow Plague ten winters ago." She shook her head. "'Twas just a foolish dream."

"No dream is foolish," Geoff told her as he released her wrist. "Not even those of departed mothers and mysterious towers." He reached into a pouch at his belt and removed a small crystal orb which he now set onto the table in front of him. He muttered something to softly to be understood and began staring into its depths.

Mikel looked at Franz, who shrugged in reply.

Kathe hurried away.

* * *

"Thou press us hard!" Mikel called out.

Geoff reined in his grey mare. "Do I?"

"Do thou know something that we do not?" Mikel demanded of him. "Knowledge of where more of these Gods-damned Chthonians lair?"

"No, of course not." Geoff shook his head. "I am merely interested in reaching the end of the journey as quickly as might be arranged. I am not one for spending overmuch time on horseback."

"Truer words were never spoken," Norvgan agreed from where he swayed precariously in his own saddle. "Horses!" he snorted. That single word was invested with considerable baggage and meaning.

"We're making good time. If thou push the horses too much, they'll die before we reach the watch towers." Franz kept his tone steady. His cloak flapped in the breeze.

Geoff nodded with some reluctance and allowed his mare to slow to a canter. "I am in no true hurry after all. No doubt the wench spoke merely of foolish dreams."

"So you say." Mikel's eyes never stopped scanning the forest. "We spent two days in the village and saw no further trace of Chthonians, nor heard tell of other dreams of anyone's *mother*."

"So ye think the danger is averted?"

"I entertain the possibility," Mikel agreed. "And yet I would not return to the capitol without first making certain. People dreamed of the Watch Towers and I will ride there."

Geoff flicked the reins of his dappled grey mare. "As ye wish."

* * *

"I have still seen little traffic on these roads." Franz took a drink from his water skin.

"There be many Goblin raids," Norvgan spat into the dirt of the hard-packed road and held his reins more tightly. "There will be convoys still coming from the mines, but they will be few and large with many stout Dwarfs to guard them."

"And lots of axes?"

"Is there any better weapon, Manling?"

A raven cawed loudly from somewhere in the trees.

"What has stirred up the Goblins?"

"Who knows." The Dwarf spat again. "They prey on wagons, despite the patrols of men and Dwarfs. They burn farms and plunder crops. They have sought to infiltrate our mines and holdings...few returned to their own warrens to tell of their defeat," he finished with a satisfied grunt.

Mikel chuckled.

Geoff was staring blankly into the distance as he rode.

"Matters should improve for ye now," Norvgan said.

"And why is that?"

"Why, because ye now have a stout Dwarf at thy side."

"True." Franz managed to keep a straight face as he agreed with the Dwarf.

"And any Dwarf is worth any three Manling warriors. No offence."

"None taken."

"Some Manlings are valiant warriors, but axe for axe, give me a Dwarf." When he was distracted and not holding tightly to the reins, Norvgan was a passable rider. "Consider the armour...none can match Dwarf forging skills. Training is another factor, Franz. I've been swinging this axe since thy grandfather was a newborn babe."

"I believe thee." Franz was nodding.

The trees gave way to stony meadow with surprising abruptness.

Franz reined in his horse. "There it is." The watchtower was built from a basic design: a wooden palisade twice the height of a man, encircling a stone tower that likely contained four or five floors. It overlooked the road, giving the garrison the ability to watch their surroundings. A banner flapped from the top of the tower.

"The watch tower seems quiet."

"Too quiet." Mikel grimaced.

"There should be lights. The smell of a cook fire." As they rode closer, Franz rested his hand on his sword. "Come, we must investigate this." He dismounted from his horse and started walking across the low-cropped grass.

"Aye, let us take them on foot." Norvgan hastily followed suit, tying the reins of his horse to a low-hanging tree branch. "There have been sheep here recently." The grass was freshly cropped.

"Tall grass just offers places for bandits to hide. The sheep make good eating later on."

The gates hung open.

"This should not be." Mikel looked around. "They should be closed at all times, and likely locked."

"There should be sentries here and on the walls. I see no one." Franz was holding his sword in a loose grip and he had pushed back his cloak to grant easy movement for his sword arm.

Geoff eyed the deserted courtyard inside the outer wall. "Very strange." He gripped his staff more tightly.

"Indeed."

Norvgan was eying the tower. "Looks like decent stone work," he commented. "Did ye hire Dwarfs to aid in the building?"

"I have no idea. These towers have been here for centuries." Built by a long-dead Baron to protect his realm from Goblins lairing in the Peaks.

"'Tis good work. Solid." He looked up. "No low windows." There were some on what was likely the tower's fourth level. "Good place for archers to shoot from."

Mikel studied the ground, but the hard-packed earth told him nothing. "Do thou sense anything, Mage?"

"No." Geoff took a deep breath. "I sense no magical presence, but the aura of this place is disturbed." He fumbled in the pockets of his robe and finally removed a red jewel. He held it up to his right eye. "There is no trace of magic."

The night was quiet.

"Nothing?"

"Nothing that I can sense." Geoff lowered the gem. "Yet something is very wrong here." The mage shook his head, looking confused. "It feels much as the farmhouse did."

"Then we must be cautious," Franz told them.

"Aye." Mikel took a grip on his sword. "Inside." He gestured towards the silent tower.

Chapter Nine

Mikel and Franz stepped through the open doorway and into single large room which formed the ground floor of the watch tower.

"Look at the rust on those hinges." Franz gestured with his left hand. "Two weeks of exposure to the rains I'd dare say."

"That long?"

"Aye."

Geoff held his staff with a firm grip and he was muttering softly to himself as he walked onto the hard-packed dirt floor. He looked around the chamber, noting the doorways which pierced the thick stone walls. "Stark," he commented. The room was lit solely by the sunlight coming through the open door. Burned-out torches hung in their sconces, dark and cold.

"It's a watch tower, not a palace." Mikel kept twisting his head, trying to see everything at once. "There should be a stable through that door." He pointed to a wide doorway. Watch towers tended to be laid out according to the same design. "Storeroom through there." He pointed to another door.

"And the stairs to the upper levels are through there?"

"Aye."

Norvgan eyed the entrance to the stairway. "No inner doors on the stairs?" he asked. "Not a very secure design." The doors to the stable and storeroom were both half-closed.

"There are doors." Franz grimaced as he hurried towards the opening. "There should be doors," he amended. "Something must have torn them loose."

Norvgan gripped his axe more tightly.

Mikel cursed softly as he looked at the stone walls where hinges had once been. He turned away from the stairs. "We check this floor first, then we shall ascend."

Franz nodded.

Norvgan took a step toward the storeroom.

"No one travels alone!" Mikel snapped quickly. "We know not what happened here and I will not risk losing anyone to ambush."

Geoff nodded. "As ye wish." He paced after Norvgan. "Be cautious, Dwarf!"

"Always, Mage." Norvgan checked inside the storeroom. "Empty," he declared over his shoulder. "Something has ransacked its way though here." There were barrels and crates, all smashed open. "They've eaten everything." He poked at one crate with the shaft of his axe.

"This could be the work of common brigands or Goblins." Geoff poked the debris with his staff.

"'Tis not befouled as Goblins would do."

"True." Geoff stepped back into the main room. "Room enough for a wagon or three in here."

"The garrison would have kept their wagons in the yard outside," Mikel replied. He was standing alone. "This room would be kept clean, save when a supply wagon was actually being unloaded."

"The storeroom is picked clean," Norvgan told him. "Not a crumb left within to feed a rat." He chuckled grimly. "There's not even a sign of a rat."

"The attackers ate the horses as well." Franz emerged from the stable, looking pale. "I've seen many battlefields, but nothing matches such a slaughterhouse as in there." He pulled the door closed behind him and leaned against it. "Ye Gods."

"Upstairs then." Mikel eyed the others. "We must venture up."

"Aye." Franz nodded reluctantly. "Though I fear what sights we will encounter."

"Lead on!" Norvgan ordered. "Or step aside."

Mikel led the way towards the opening, eying yet again the marked stone where the missing hinges had been. "It will be darker up here. There are no windows until we reach the upper floors."

"Darkness does not bother me." Norvgan took the lead with some eagerness. "Reminds me of the tunnels of home." He began to climb the stairs.

"Can't we kindle a torch?"

"These are long burned out." Geoff tapped one. "There be nothing left to burn I fear."

The second floor was divided into rooms.

"Another storeroom," Norvgan reported. "Ransacked and empty."

"The kitchen is equally barren." Franz was holding a flickering candle as he stepped into the mess shall. "There be evidence of meals left." All three tables had plates and overturned goblets and mugs and the stench of decay was strong. "The garrison was plainly surprised."

"Aye." Norvgan grimaced. "But what could have taken them so quickly?" he asked. "And why no evidence of battle below? Even taken by surprise, Manlings will fight."

Mikel emerged from another room, holding his own candle. "There be no evidence of battle here, yet plainly something took place here. Else where has the garrison gone?" He shook his head. "Have ye some thought, Mage?"

Geoff turned. "Thy pardon?"

"I asked if ye had some thought as to the disappearance of the garrison?"

"Nay, I do not." Geoff was staring at the floor. He was not holding any candle, but he could see well enough.

"What do ye see?" Franz asked.

"Nothing of import. Merely the weathering of the stones."

"Stones do not weather on the *inside* of a tower," Norvgan told him. He pushed past the mage. "Let us continue to ascend."

There was some light shining down the stairwell.

"There should be dormitories on the third level." Franz grunted as the toe of his boot caught on a step. "Would that we had more light. This candle is all but spent. Mage, can ye not cast a spell? Geoff?"

The mage had stopped climbing and was staring at the wall.

The grey stone walls had been changed in appearance and the travellers stopped to look.

Norvgan tapped the wall with the blade of his axe. "What foul sorcery is this?" he demanded.

"Some trick of which I know little." Face pale, Geoff touched it. "The very nature of the stones is changed." They appeared to have been covered in some secretion that hung in loops and coils, turning the corridors into the petrified innards of some beast. "This is most unusual."

"It continues up."

"Aye." Norvgan grunted. "It feels moist in here."

"Like a swamp?"

"Aye."

"Do ye see anything?" Mikel asked as they reached the top of the stairs and entered a long corridor.

"Nay. 'Tis too dark." Franz dropped his extinguished candle. "Norvgan, is there enough—"

A rattling hiss sounded from the shadows.

The adventurers froze.

A shadow moved.

"*Lumous*!" A ball of light flared into being above the mage.

The shadow took on substance as the light glinted wetly on its greenish carapace.

"By the Gods!"

The creature was taller than any of them, with no apparent eyes in its elongated head. Its body was impossibly thin, and its limbs were tipped with claws. A double row of arm-length spikes traced out its spine and tail.

"What is that thing?" Mikel demanded as he watched its twitching tail lash back and forth.

"Another demon."

The creature opened its double jaws and hissed. Thick slime dripped from its fangs to splatter onto the flagstone floor.

Geoff froze.

The creature skittered forward with insect-like agility.

"Damn it!" Mikel lunged forward and swung his sword. He grunted as he lopped the elongated head from the demon's thin neck.

Greenish ichors splattered across the grey stones of the wall.

"A very nice blow, lad." Norvgan grunted approvingly as he studied the body. "Very nice indeed. At last we can see what our foe looks like without the mage having first fried it to a blackened crsip."

"Disgusting things." Mikel spat onto the floor. "I think we might guess at the fate of the garrison here." He shook his head. "The poor devils likely knew not what attacked them."

"By the Gods!" Franz exclaimed. "Mikel!"

"What?"

"Thy sword!"

"By the Gods!" Mikel dropped the hilt and stared in horror as the blade continued to dissolve. *What if I had sheathed it?* he thought in horror.

"It was the demon's blood." The mage studied the still-dissolving blade and then looked at the stones of the wall. "A most potent acid indeed." They were hissing and smoking as the stone was being eaten away.

"How do we fight such a beast?" Mikel demanded. "If we strike it down, its own blood will slay us."

"Don't get splashed." Norvgan shrugged. "Seems a fair strategy."

"But our weapons will be consumed with the first blow!" Mikel drew his dagger and laughed bitterly at the thought of fending off another demon with such a short-bladed weapon. "No wonder the garrison failed to survive such an ambush."

"But how did these things come to be here?"

"This will require more research." Geoff bent his head towards the bubbling stone, moving the light from his staff in closer. "It loses potency with time. The decay is slowing."

"So this one's death won't bring the whole tower crashing down on our heads?"

"No, Franz, I don't think so."

"That's good to know." Norvgan was eying the tower. "Good solid construction, as I said earlier."

Franz pointed. "Look there. The demon is not dissolving."

"Ye are right." Geoff nodded. "They are immune to their blood."

"As is the shell covering the stones." Norvgan tapped a piece. "'Tis very much like the scales of the dragon."

"I should take a piece of each for study."

Mikel looked away from the mage. "These demons are truly hellish creatures. What kind of beast would have such potent blood?"

"I am surprised that we have not witnessed this before," Franz commented. His brown eyes narrowed and he suddenly looked at the mage. "But then I recall that we have not slain a demon yet...Geoff has slain each that we have yet faced. Save this last."

Geoff straightened. "Aye," he said, "and as these things prove to be even more deadly in death than in life, perhaps it is best that I handle them with my magic."

"I place more trust in steel than sorcery," Mikel replied.

Geoff glanced down that pitted sword hilt lying on the acid-etched stones. He made no comment.

Mikel grunted.

Norvgan snorted. "I hate to tell ye, but we're surrounded." He hefted his axe and tightened his grip on it.

More of the green-shelled creatures were gathering at the end of the corridor. Viscous slime dripped from their jaws.

"What do we do?"

"We fight or we die." Franz tightened his grip on his sword. "I know which I choose." He charged down the corridor with a battle cry. "For the Baroness!" His swung his sword and cut loose the arm from one of the creatures, then immediately followed with another cut to slice off the beast's head. He dodged back hastily to avoid the splash of greenish blood which splattered the walls. "We must be swift!" He gave his sword a sharp flick to loosen the blood from it, but the blade was already acid-etched.

"Aye, we fight." Norvgan swung his axe and the blade chopped the legs out from under one beast. A second blow cut off its head. "I claim fair blood price!"

Geoff blinked as the Dwarf struck down another demon and then another. "How is that thou can fight it?" he asked in shock.

"Rune-marked blade. Magically hardened." The Dwarf smiled at him, a fierce light in his eyes. "Can cut through anything with this." He turned back towards another demon. "Taste Dwarf steel monster!"

The beast hissed.

Mikel shook his head helplessly. "I need more than my dagger!"

Geoff lifted his staff. "Get out of the way, fool Dwarf!" he shouted. "Anything I cast will strike thee as well!"

Norvgan pushed his way around a corner, still bellowing harsh-sounding Dwarfish curses.

Franz sliced through another demon with his blade, tearing open its chest. "Gah!" he shrieked as greenish blood splashed across his face and chest. "Ahh!" He staggered backwards and fell back onto the floor, sword clattering away from his hand.

"Franz!" Mikel ran to his side.

More demons skittered down the corridor, clinging to the walls and ceiling with their claws.

"I banish you!" Geoff hurled lightning bolts into their midst. "Back into the abyss, thou foul creatures!"

The last of the Chthonians had fallen and Geoff leaned heavily on his ash staff. "Ye Gods, that was too much." The air was heavy with a stench that combined brimstone with a burning middenheap. "Norvgan?"

"A moment longer!" the Dwarf yelled back.

"We have slain them all," Geoff said and turned his head. "Mike—ye Gods!"

Franz was moaning softly, unconscious. The burns were raw and oozing. Most of his face was bare bone and his tunic was rotted away.

"Can't thou heal him, Mage?" Mikel demanded from where he knelt next to his friend. "Do something!" he pleaded.

"Ye Gods." Geoff shook his head sadly. "Healing is not one of my talents."

"Ye must try!"

Geoff moved closer, then closed his eyes for a moment and murmured something under his breath.

Norvgan returned from checking the uppermost level. "No sign of any more of those damned beasts. I think we slew the lot of them." A bloody scratched marked his face and there were a few sizzling spots on his chain mail, but otherwise he was unharmed. "There's a lot of bones up there though," he said leaning on his axe. "A lot of bones...."

Mikel said nothing.

Franz was moaning now.

"Gods of the Deep." Norvgan cursed.

"You're not a very good mage." Mikel had laid his own cloak over his fallen friend. He looked up at Geoff with tears streaming down his cheeks. "Do something!"

"I have done what I can." Geoff spread his hands helplessly. "I cannot heal him of these wounds."

"Then what good are you?"

"He is a fake."

Geoff froze as Norvgan spoke up.

"He is a fake." The Dwarf watched him closely, his axe held in his hands. "I have seen many mages in my travels and I know the signs of a true master of the arcane arts. He lacks them."

Mikel stood up. "Is this truth?" he asked softly.

Geoff said nothing.

"Is this *true*?" Mikel grabbed the mage's robes. "By all the Gods, I led my friend into battle in the belief that thou knew what thou were doing!"

"I didn't know it would be like this." Geoff was plainly shaken. "By the Gods, I had no idea we would face this nest!"

Mikel threw the mage roughly against the wall and the white ash staff rattled across the floor. "Have thee no magic?"

"I have some talents," Geoff said haughtily. "Though not enough to be a proper Battle Mage," he admitted. "My staff was built to aid in focusing my latent abilities."

"Great." Mikel turned away. "We are facing a threat to the entire barony and thou have no real magic?"

"I didn't say that. I have researched many legends, as my Master did before me. I hope to find an answer in the Great Library."

"Damn you!" Mikel dropped to his knees again. "He's dying." He stared at Franz's ruined face. "He's dying!"

"I—I can do nothing to cure him." Geoff shrugged helplessly. He bent to pick up his staff.

"I have some salves in my pack."

"Dwarf salves will be of little aid to a Human," Mikel told him bitterly.

"I do have a potion." Geoff was holding a small phial in his hand, which he had retrieved from a pocket in his robes. "It will not cure Franz of such a grievous injury. But it will...ease him into sleep."

Mikel eyed the phial and the mage. "Sleep?" he asked.

"Aye." Geoff's face was pale as he swallowed. "The eternal sleep."

Mikel's eyes widened. "Thou want to poison him?"

"He is already dead! This will remove his pain."

"Damn you, Mage." Mikel looked back down at his friend, tears streaming down his cheeks. "And damn me as well."

Chapter Ten

"The barony is growing ever more restless." Baroness Carolinka frowned at the other people in the chamber. They stood gathered in small groups: mages, priests, and a few of her most favoured and trusted courtiers. *They do not mingle. They stand in opposition to one another, drawing up as if for battle.* It was a disturbing thought.

Bells chimed elsewhere in the castle.

Two servants stood back near the doors, out of the way, yet close enough to run should something be required.

Carolinka resisted the urge to pace. It was a small room, the available floor space dominated by a single table. The bowls of fruit and mugs of wine were ignored, just as no one looked at the bright tapestries on the walls. "People are having nightmares. Dreams of a *dark Mother* and a ruined city."

"Terrible things."

"Aye, how do thou protect against a dream?"

Carolinka was wearing a revealing gown of yellow, slashed with white, and her hair was loosely tied back in a yellow ribbon. "That is why I have summoned thee, Pavel. Thou, and thy fellows, are learned mages. Prove thy worth to me."

The man with longest beard offered a bow. "We shall do our best, my Lady. Yet for all of our arts, we are at a loss."

"This is a matter for the Gods."

"Indeed, Revered One." Josem voiced his agreement in a respectful tone of voice. His yellow and orange robes were spotless and he stood behind the ancient priest. They, and the other four priests wore small silver bells in their beards and hair. "Thy words are simple truth."

The old priest nodded his head slowly, his bells tinkling softly. "This is a time of trial and testing for us all," he intoned. "The Gods frown upon the corruption of the world. These manifestations are but a sign of their disfavour with us."

"Hardly." Pavel gestured dismissively with his ring-bedecked hand. "These are simply magic gone astray. They might even be considered as a quasi-natural phenomena."

"Oh, indeed? Typical of a mage...ignore the hints of the Gods in favour of thy own importance."

"Thy Temple is richly appointed," Pavel pointed out, his green eyes narrowing. "The statues and trappings of thy supposed servants are richer than we wear."

"Enough!" Carolinka grimaced. "Mages and priests alike...I have need of thy services. This is a time of crisis and the barony is in danger. The city seethes with unrest and discontent. My Guardsmen are loyal," she nodded to her captain of the Guard, "yet they are unable to restore and maintain a lasting order. Ordering them into the streets with drawn blades is but asking for further trouble and riots."

The narrow-faced man nodded his agreement. "Though I do not fear a battle, my Lady, there is no honour to be won in facing down a street riot." Gavin grimaced. "Indeed, it would be a bloody slaughter and the Guards would be stained worse than the streets. The first battle would be but a herald of things to come and all would suffer."

"Thank you, Captain." Carolinka turned towards the priests.

"The Baroness is correct, these are times for caution." The Revered One pursed his lips tightly. His bells tinkled.

"Your forgiveness for my rash outburst." Pavel offered her a shallow bow. "We spoke without thinking."

The doors to the chamber burst open and the two servants jumped.

Gavin reached for his sword, but arrested the motion as Geoff scurried in, followed by a scowling Mikel and a Dwarf. All three wore tattered clothing, and the dust of the road.

Carolinka eyed them all in concern. "Mikel, I was not aware that thou had returned." She studied him again, noting the lines on his face and the state of his attire. "Thou has come with important news for me then?"

"This so-called *mage* does." Mikel rested his hand on his sheathed dagger and glared at the mage. He was unshaven and unsteady on his feet. "Speak, Geoff."

"I have little to say at this time." Geoff eyed the other mages who were in the room and he hastily attempted to straighten his bronze robes and ragged beard. "Mikel, thou can give the Baroness a far more accurate account of things." He fell silent and eyed the dagger as Mikel slowly drew it from its sheath. "Or perhaps I should speak then."

The gathered mages stared at him with mingled surprise and confusion on their faces.

Guardsmen and servants stood in the open doorway, staring into the room.

Geoff's hand tightened on his ash staff.

"Someone must speak!" Carolinka shook her head. "The people are growing more worried. The Dark Mother's influence grows daily. I do not know how much longer my guardsmen can contain the violence."

Gavin grimaced. "The swords of the Guard stand ready to serve thee, Baroness, but will our steel avail us against these demons which are rumoured to stalk the northern villages?"

"That is what we must learn, Gavin. Magic and religion alike must act to safeguard the city, even if the citizens do not see the need."

The Guardsman nodded.

Carolinka's gaze again drifted over to Mikel. "Well?"

He gestured at Geoff. "Speak, Mage."

Geoff winced at the harsh tone in Mikel's voice. "My master was the Mage Conrad. I trained under him for many years, apprenticed in the common manner." He exchanged looks with Pavel, who frowned. "Last summer, he arranged to purchase something...he told me they were dragon eggs."

Carolinka blinked at that.

"He was using them for experiments, but I do not know what the purpose of them was. I was forbidden to enter certain portions of his tower. This is not uncommon practice among Mages, so I was not concerned."

"That is true," one of the other mages agreed in a deep voice. "An apprentice cannot be exposed to the full arcane mysteries too soon. Such knowledge would corrupt them and sear their minds."

Josem grimaced and shook his head, the single bell in his beard ringing softly. "Corruption comes as the cost of meddling with powers meant for the Gods alone."

"Peace!" Carolinka pleaded. "Geoff, please continue."

"It was in the cellar catacombs. I was forbidden to pass beyond certain doors. Conrad spent much time down there, immersed in his rituals and spells. He had tasks for me to oversee and accomplish so I was kept busy and away from the supposed dragon eggs.

"There were screams from the cellars one night. Terrible screams." Geoff shuddered at the memory. "In the morning, I encountered Conrad in the tower's library.

"My Master was changed...he seemed darker. Drained of his humour, dark as it often was, and more...." He shook his head. "It was shortly after that the Mother began speaking to me in my dreams."

"What was in the cellar?"

Geoff shook his head. "I cannot speak of it."

"What was in the cellar?" Carolinka demanded a second time.

"It's a nest," Mikel guessed. His voice had turned cold. "Like the one we entered in the watch tower?"

Geoff said nothing.

"He has spoken the truth to us." Pavel and his fellows exchanged looks. "We would know if he lied."

"But would ye tell us?" Josem demanded.

"What of Beaudral?"

"We fought Chthonians there." Mikel tossed a piece of parchment onto the table. "Franz sketched one. Before he..." He bit his lower lip.

"And where is Franz?" Carolinka frowned. "I would have expected him to be with thee."

Mikel shook his head and stared at the floor.

Geoff flinched and stared at his white-knuckled hand gripping his staff.

"He died a warrior's death," Norvgan told them all in a calm voice. "Fighting Chthonians in the watch tower at Crooked Stream."

"*Chthonians?*" Carolinka asked. "Again ye speak this name. What manner of foe bears such a title?"

"Terrible beasts" the Dwarf replied. "Dragons loosed from the Infernal Realms. That sketch does them little justice."

Carolinka unrolled the parchment and looked at it. Her faced paled.

Mikel shook his head. "We slew many of the things," he said brokenly. "Both near Beaudral, and at the watch tower...but I fear more remain loose."

"I know nothing of creatures that look thus." Pavel handed the parchment to his fellows. "This is no natural dragon. Though there are legends, perhaps, of similar beasts once sighted stalking their prey."

"Ye speak of legends and myths." Josem dropped the parchment back onto the table and barely managed to suppress a shudder before it made his bell ring. "These are clearly matters more serious than we had first assumed. If thou name them as hellish beasts, then are they truly demonic?"

Geoff nodded. "Aye."

The priests exchanged looks. "Thou named them, Mage?"

"My Master did, Revered One."

"After the Nostronomun legends?"

Carolinka frowned at Josem's question.

Pavel nodded his head slowly. "I am certain that Conrad had his reasons for doing so." His green eyes locked gazes with Geoff and the younger mage flinched, then hastily looked away.

"No doubt."

"A name is useful, as is the sketch." Carolinka shuddered before tossing the parchment back onto the table. "But this solves little of our problem. Are there truly more of these things?"

"Geoff believes so." Norvgan was leaning on his axe.

"We found a nest of these creatures lairing near Beaudral. They had taken refuge in an abandoned farmhouse cellar." Mikel frowned. "Geoff cleared it out with his magic."

Geoff clutched his staff more tightly.

"Then we stopped near a watch tower, near the Shadow Peaks, and found that it had been overrun. The garrison was dead and there were a lot of Chthonians there." His voice broke. "We cleansed that nest too."

"Two nests, Norvgan, thou claim to have cleansed," the Baroness said. "But how many others remain?" She looked at the mage.

Geoff shook his head.

"So we could have an unknown number of nests of these demonic creatures lairing within my barony?" Carolinka sounded horrified. "By the Gods, how can this be?"

Pavel frowned. "A better question would be 'what can we do about the ones here'?"

"First I would ban the traffic in dragon eggs." Gavin made that comment in a low tone.

"Ban them?" Pavel kept his voice civil, but his eyebrows rose. "Do ye know how rare and precious they are?"

"Aye. Very rare, very precious." The Guardsman nodded. "And very dangerous!"

"Only to fools. The College must have access to eggs for certain rituals, but ye cannot ban them entirely."

"It seems reasonable to me."

"Would ye ban all implements of magic, Josem?"

The priest nodded. "Aye, if I could."

"Bah!" Pavel snorted. "Ye are a fool then. Magic has a rightful place in this world."

"I want the trade in these eggs halted."

"Far easier said, then implanted, Baroness." Gavin shook his head with obvious reluctance. "We cannot search every traveller."

"The College will protest such a ban," Pavel warned her, "and your captain is correct. Such a ban cannot be enforced."

"If a single egg and one rogue mage can cause such misery and suffering onto my barony, then I cannot tolerate such risks in the future."

"These are not normal eggs and not normal dragons." Pavel gestured to the parchment. "This is a matter which requires considerably more discussion and debate." He drew himself up to his full height. "We shall retire to the College and question our apprentice in greater detail."

"I am not finished with my own questions."

"Ye have thy cousin and the Dwarf." Pavel turned on his heel. "We shall send word when we have come to some consensus." The mages filed out of the room after him.

The priests murmured amongst themselves.

Gavin watched them go, resting his hand on his sword. "Shall I—"

"No, let them go." Carolinka watched them. "Let Pavel have his moment. Mikel, tell me all that you know."

Chapter Eleven

Mikel stood on the balcony of one of the eastern towers. He was staring across the night-darkened city. *It looks so peaceful. The people do not know what horrors lurk in the night, what dangers have been unleashed upon the barony.* The wind tugged at his green cloak.

"Thy warning comes at a good time."

Mikel did not turn at the sound of the voice, or the tinkling of the bell.

Josem stepped closer. "The mage spoke in great detail of the battle at the watch tower."

Mikel was gripping the railing so tightly that his knuckles were white. "Did he also tell thee how he lied to us?"

"He did not lie."

"He's a fake!"

"The College of Mages has already taken him aside to be chastised."

"Chastised. *Chastised*?" Mikel shouted. Tears were running freely down his cheeks. "I trusted him and so did Franz. And now...now Franz is dead."

Josem flinched. "He is with the Gods." He attempted to sound soothing, though he doubted that he was succeeding.

"He was killed by those demons...and by that Gods-damned mage."

"Geoff was of use to thee in all of thy battles," Josem forced himself to speak the words in a calm tone. "Thou would likely not have succeeded in cleansing the nests without his magic to aid thee."

"We had the Dwarf's axe."

"Thou will need more than that, or so it appears." He approached closer. "Grieve now. There is no shame in tears for a beloved comrade."

Mikel shook his head and wiped his eyes. "There is no time," he replied in a weary tone. "The council of war will be meeting in a few minutes. I must be there."

"I will be there as well...but do not take too much onto thy shoulders. Thou will do no honour to Franz's memory should thou also be killed foolishly."

"I will do what I must."

* * *

Carolinka stared at the map which had been unrolled and covered most of the oak table. "Conrad's tower is here." Her finger tapped a mark.

"Aye." Geoff had been very quiet since his revelations in the grand hall. Pavel stood at his side, looking grim.

Josem stood on the far side the table. "The bulk of the Mother's Cult has been concentrated in the surrounding villages, outside of the capitol."

"Places such as Beaudral."

"Aye."

Pavel paced back to the cluster of mages standing near the north window. Seven cloaked men and women had accompanied him, several of whom still wore their cowls pulled up to mask their identity.

"I have sent patrols there, but they have encountered none of these Chthonians." Gavin gestured to the map. He wore no armour, but he was wearing the puffy-sleeved jacket of the Guards.

Mikel entered the room. "How many patrols have thou heard from?" His eyes were red and he smelled strongly of wine. His tunic and breeches were clean though.

The Baroness's eyes narrowed. "Ten patrols were sent; ten patrols have reported back to me."

"Recently?"

"Riders have come to me within the last quarter-moon."

Mikel shook his head. "What did they find?" He reached for a goblet of wine from a tray a servant was holding.

"Frightened villagers." Josem spoke up. He was the sole priest to attend this meeting. "The same as my Brothers. The Revered One has dispatched many to comfort the frightened and root out this Cult. Some of them have failed to report back," he admitted. "Others have reported abandoned farms."

"These things are spreading."

"But slowly."

Pavel murmured something softly to a female mage who nodded.

Carolinka grimaced. "Slowly or not, this is unacceptable. They must be rooted out and exterminated."

Mikel studied the map.

Gavin placed white stones onto the map in half a dozen spots. "My men have skirmished with groups of cultists at these places."

"And we have encountered them here." Josem added his own round grey stones. "Or so we have heard from messenger doves."

"They seem to be concentrated in one part of the countryside."

"For now."

"And that very concentration now reveals them." Clad in clean bronze robes, and looking extremely tired, Geoff emerged from the cluster of mages and strode across the room. "The pattern of attacks forms a ring around Conrad's tower."

Mikel looked coldly at Geoff. "Well, Mage? Have thou more to offer than simply that?"

Geoff chewed at his lip, then he stood erect and held his staff in a firm grip. "It would appear that the Chthonians are nesting within my master's abode."

"Do thou still have loyalty to him?" Carolinka asked.

"No." Geoff shook his head and answered in a firm tone of voice. "He has perverted the Arcane Wisdoms for his own gain. He has turned his back on the Gods." The young mage shivered. "He has violated every teaching and belief that mages are sworn to live by."

"Mages can seldom be trusted," Josem pointed out sourly. "They tamper with divine powers best left to the Gods."

"Spare us thy usual tired drivel." Pavel's eyes narrowed. "We use magic in the same manner as thy priests."

"We pray for guidance from the Gods. We channel their powers as they grant us boons. Mages steal their powers for their own advancement."

"Magic is there for the taking!"

"Enough!"

Geoff flinched at the sound of Carolinka's voice.

She glared at everyone. Few were used to hearing such harshness. "We lack the time and grace to argue openly amongst ourselves. The cult grows in strength and these demons multiply. They must be stopped. They must be rooted out and destroyed."

"We need to destroy their nest." Mikel spoke in a low tone and refused to look at the clustered mages. "We must destroy the nest."

"Conrad's tower?"

"It must be razed."

The mages looked displeased while Josem was smiling.

"Agreed." Carolinka nodded. "Mikel, thou will lead my army."

Mikel said nothing.

"Gavin, thou will accompany him as troop captain."

"As ye wish, my Lady." Gavin nodded. "I'll have Guardsmen ready to march in two days." He offered her a bow.

"Take a quarter moon to prepare thyselves. The army must march quickly, but thou *must* march to victory. Preparation now will aid thee later in the battle to come."

"Yes, Baroness."

"A little delay will help towards victory, but tarry too long and it will only go ill for us. These demons must be slain before they can spread their evil still further."

"I will send word to my brothers," Josem said. "This battle will require more than ordinary steel if we are to overcome this foe."

Geoff paled.

* * *

Mikel swung his sword with a blank expression on his face while he practiced the ancient forms on the hard-packed dirt of the practice yard. He was clean-shaven and dressed in a clean, though roughly woven, tunic.

Men-at-arms watched him.

"Those demons are fast," Norvgan said from where he was sitting atop a barrel. "Fast and deadly." He watched the swinging blade. "They have claws and fangs that tear through plate armour as if it was paper."

Gavin winced at the description. "So how do we slay such a beast?"

"By being faster." The Dwarf slid his thumb along the edge of his axe. "And ye must be fast cause the beast's blood is a most potent acid. One splash will burn through both armour and flesh."

Gavin turned pale. "We must consider this," he said, "and choose our weapons carefully." He rubbed at his breastplate as if already envisioning the metal melting away.

"Arrows from afar would be thy best hope. Slay them long before they can reach thee."

"They can die," Mikel announced coldly. "And we're going to kill them."

"Aye, lad." Norvgan hopped to the ground. "That we will."

* * *

Mikel hurried through the market, without hearing the cries of the hawkers and the haggling of shoppers. His dark green cloak flapped in the breeze as he hurried forward on foot, having eschewed his horse. "So soon?" he muttered as the store came into view.

The door of the tailor shop was closed.

"Gods grant me strength." With a trembling hand, he reached up and knocked. Then he tugged at his tunic collar to loosen it.

Moments passed.

Mikel knocked again.

A pair of men-at-arms walked past him. They nodded to him and he nodded back.

"Isn't she at home?" Mikel knocked more loudly. "I know that she is growing deaf, but surely she must hear something." A sudden gust of wind tugged at his cloak. "Perhaps she is around the back."

The alleyway was not cobbled. He had to turn sideways to slide his way between the two houses—they were all built very close together in this old neighbourhood—and the smell was foul. "Worse than burning Chthonians," he muttered, almost gagging as his boot squished something.

Mikel reached a gate and pushed at it. It opened into a small garden.

The scent of lavender was strong in the air.

He walked past the flourishing herbs and towards the back of the house. Like many shopkeepers, Helga lived atop her store, with a separate entrance at the back. This door was unlatched.

"Hello?" Mikel called out. "Seamstress Helga?"

The house was silent.

"Perhaps she sleeps." Or perhaps she had gone out on some errand. "I could return here later. Or leave her a note." But he was unable to turn away from the door. "Damn me for a coward!" he swore. "I cannot do this. I hate this foul duty, but it is my task alone." He pushed the door open and stepped into a small cloakroom. "Hello?"

The inner door swung open into a kitchen. Flowers filled vases, and lined the worn oak table, shelves hanging on the plastered walls, and the windowsill.

The old woman was sitting in a chair, facing the window.

"Forgive my intrusion, Mistress." Mikel paused and swallowed. The scent of flowers was almost overwhelming and he sneezed. *Franz told me she was losing her sense of smell.* "Helga, it's me, Mikel. Franz's friend?" Perhaps she was dozing. "I've come with news of thy son." Reluctantly, he reached towards her shoulder. "Ill news, I fear. Franz is..." his voice trailed off.

The woman in the chair was dead.

Chapter Twelve

"That damned mage is in hiding."

"He is not 'in hiding', Mikel. He has spent the last quarter-moon in the library." Carolinka was wearing a ruby-red dress as they walked into a room filled with shelves and racks containing hundreds of books and scrolls. Her hair was pulled back, and coiled tightly in a severe fashion. "He is making no effort not to be found. Dozens have seen him today alone." Lanterns were hung along the walls, giving a warm light to the room.

Mikel snorted.

Ignoring him, Carolinka continued walking, an entourage of a dozen people following her.

Gavin glanced at him, then followed her. Even here in the heart of the castle, he wore breastplate and helmet, and carried his sword at his waist.

At length, Mikel followed her. He wore no sword, but a dagger was sheathed at his waist and he wore a grey tunic and black breeches. His boots were loud on the stone floor.

They rounded a corner and spotted a man with his head resting on a parchment laden table.

"Thou sleep?"

Geoff started at Mikel's question and he almost fell from his chair. Several scrolls rolled from the table to fall to the floor as he rose unsteadily to his feet. "I, I was researching the ancient myths and legends." The mage's robes were wrinkled and stained with past meals. His eyes were bloodshot and he looked haggard. Even his red beard was ragged and untrimmed.

"What legends?" Carolinka asked while Mikel grimaced silently. "The Nostronomun ones?"

"Aye, my Lady." Geoff attempted to smooth out his bronze robes, without success.

"And what have thou learned?"

"The Nostronomuns left numerous drawings and records which have been retrieved by adventurers over the years." He tapped one of his thin fingers against an illustration in the book he had been sleeping on. "That looks very much like our demon."

Mikel looked closer. "Aye, it does."

Carolinka shivered. "Such a beast." The blue ink drawing captured the full malevolence of the beast. Six-fingered claw-tipped hands raised to strike, fang-filled mouth gaping open, and it seemed poised to leap from the page and attack.

"The scrolls are quite specific about how deadly they are. Demonically bred insects of a sort, who nest near their prey and take on characteristics of their hosts."

"Hosts?"

"According to records, these demons hatch from eggs as some form of larvae...and then incubate inside a living host. They emerge after several days and quickly grow to their full size."

"Does the host survive this...incubation?"

"No." Geoff shook his head grimly.

Carolinka winced. "So these things...."

"Are breeding. A nest is the wrong term...they hive."

"But what lays the eggs?"

Geoff cocked his head. "The scrolls mention a demonic mother...the centre of the hive."

Carolinka frowned. "So how do we stop them?"

Geoff shook his head sadly. "The Nostronomuns failed to stop them. They were slaughtered and their empire fell."

Mikel grimaced. "Yet the demons survived."

"Apparently some of their eggs did."

Gavin cleared his throat. "Surely not every Nostronomun was killed," he said softly. "Someone survived to write those scrolls. Someone started the stories of the Fall."

"Which led to the legends we now know only too well."

Geoff unrolled one ancient scroll and cleared his throat. "Most of the citizens perished when the city-states were overrun. It is written that the demons bred quickly in the isolated areas of the Western Isles and that they came as a swarm across the heartlands." He coughed. "I can quote you from the text. 'They came as a black tide of death, nightmares given deadly life, now set loose to slaughter and kill.' Few survived their passing."

"And what few remained to escape."

"Aye...it would appear so."

"But what happened to the demons? Are they still living on the Western Islands?" Mikel asked. "Is that the danger people talk of?"

"I do not believe so. I believe they are dead...but apparently their eggs remain viable."

"And thy Master Conrad obtained one?"

"I told you already that he obtained what he was told to be a dragon's egg. He took it into his cellar and used it as part of his magic."

"Where did he get the egg?"

"From a passing traveller. I never caught his name. I was just an apprentice, of no importance to them." Geoff shrugged. "He arrived one afternoon and sought an audience with my master. I thought that he would be sent away at once, yet the note I carried seemed to surprise Conrad and he bade me bring the man into his sanctum."

Gavin shook his head. "If someone ventured into the ruins of Talrickia and was infected by those demons...."

"He would be dead."

"But this traveller was not. So why is he wandering the land and sharing out these cursed eggs? Why is he alive and not dead?"

"I do not know."

Carolinka grimaced. "Ludwig, send word to the College of Mages about this. I want to know precisely what they do with these dragon eggs."

"Of course." The aide bowed to her.

"Ordinary dragons are bad enough...but to trifle with these demonic beasts seems the sum of madness to me."

"Aye."

"Geoff, you have done well to learn so much and so quickly."

He blushed. "My masters would think so. They have all but forbidden me to further practice magic...I have overmuch time for reading."

"Pavel has some sense then," Mikel muttered.

Carolinka frowned. "Did the legends tell of means by which these demons might be banished back into the Infernal Realms?"

"Nay, I have come across no such incantations. If such an answer rests within these walls, it will take more time to discover it." He gestured to the rows of laden shelves. "Assuming that such an answer does rest here."

"My ancestors have laboured to build a mighty library, filled with knowledge from across the world. My scribes will be at thy disposal to aid in searching out the old legends."

"Word might be sent to the Revered One as well," Gavin suggested, "for the Temple archives are also extensive."

"Yes, Mikel, I want you to go personally to the Revered One and ask for his aid. He will trust thee."

Mikel nodded. "As ye wish."

"And what of the College? Do thy fellow mages know more of the legends then Pavel has yet shared?"

"I am limited in my access to those records." Geoff shrugged, looking abashed. "I am far from the most trusted apprentice at the moment."

"I will send word in any event. The College maintains extensive records and surely they will not risk these demons spreading unchecked across the land."

* * *

Columns of black smoke were rising from at least a dozen locations across the city.

Mikel stepped through the doorway. "Fires?" he asked.

Carolinka was standing at the edge of the balcony and staring at the columns. "Riots." She made the word the harshest of curses. The wind blew through her loose hair.

"The Cult?"

"What else? That damnable Cult of the Mother is spreading." Her hands clenched into fists and rested on the carved stone rail "In the last few days, Gavin has been forced to dispatch most of the Guards into the streets to maintain order. He will have fewer men to send north with thou when thou leave."

Standing beside his cousin, Mikel stared towards the columns of smoke. "Can't the priests do something?"

"They are doing what they can, but the Cult is insidious. It is spreading its tendrils faster than Josem and the others can cut them off."

"And the mages are of no use." Mikel spoke bitterly.

"The College can hardly be of us in subduing a riot. I do not wish to see my capitol burned to the ground." Her dark eyes drifted towards the distant spires of the College. "Although I would like to see some sign of support from the mages."

Mikel followed her gaze. *I see neither riots nor fires nearby to their towers,* he thought bitterly. "Thou can't trust mages. Lies and treachery are second nature to them."

The Baroness looked at him. "Not every mage is a blackheart."

"So thou believe."

"Thou trusted Geoff once, if ye chose to ride with him from Beaudral to the Shadow Peaks."

"And I was betrayed!" Mikel pointed out. "By an untalented apprentice whose own master began this mess."

Chapter Thirteen

"Why struggle?" the woman asked the terrified pottery merchant. Her loose blonde hair was dirty and her eyes were lit by inner madness. "The Mother will eagerly welcome thou into her warm and smothering embrace." The rest of her entourage nodded their heads slowly in unison.

"Please, leave us alone." The merchant took a step backwards, pressing back against his wife.

The smiling woman took a step closer to them, followed by the rest of her band. "The Mother loves you. Thou will feel the warmth of her love when thou bear her blessed children."

"Take your cult and get out of my store!"

"Thou must listen to Danica," one of the ragged men announced. "She hears the Mother's voice."

"Yes, and thou must submit to the Mother's will."

"Get out!" The merchant hefted a club, scowling and attempting to look fierce. "Out I say!"

Danica shook her head sadly. "Violence is not the answer, my deluded and lonely friend."

The merchant gave the club a swing. "Get out of my—hey!"

One of the cultists had slipped forward and now he grabbed the club from the merchant's hand.

"Bring them." Once again Danica's face broke into a happy smile as her fellows grabbed the merchant and his wife. "Bring them both back to the household." She turned and walked into the street. "The Mother calls for them." The otherwise deserted street.

"Please, just let us go," the merchant's wife pleaded.

"Do not cry. Soon thou will feel thy Mother's love." Danica gestured. "Bring them quickly now. The Mother waits."

"No!" the merchant cried out. "Someone!"

"Gag him," Danica ordered. "He will need his breath later"

"Leave them alone!" another voice shouted.

The cultists turned to look up the street as a Guardsmen hurried towards them.

"Hello, Gavin." The woman smiled calmly at the Guards. "The Mother will embrace thou all!"

Gavin frowned, his face mostly hidden by the faceguards of his conical helmet. "Danica, I must place thee under arrest." A dozen men-at-arms stood at his sides.

"Throw down thy arms and feel the love of the Mother!"

Gavin shook his head. "Arrest them." He gestured with his gauntleted hand and men-at-arms advanced on the ragged cultists. "Be gentle with them for they know not what they do."

"For the Mother!" Danica screamed. She hefted a thick wooden staff and her fellows surged towards the Guards.

"Try to take them alive!" Gavin ordered.

* * *

Geoff stared into the crystal orb.

A ghostly image wavered in front of his eyes.

Geoff blinked.

Conrad was looking back at him with a disapproving expression on his narrow face. His eyes were half-closed, but his mouth was moving silently.

"I know, Master, that I have failed to learn the lessons thou tried to teach me." Geoff kept his voice low as he spoke to the apparition. A fountain bubbled nearby, and birds chirped in the birch trees of the park forming an odd counterpoint to his conversation. "I will try to do better."

The ghostly image faded away.

Geoff sighed. *Another disappoint to thee, Master?* he thought bitterly. *I am far from the perfect apprentice I know.*

"Thou look lost."

Geoff looked up from the now cloudy sphere. The park was no longer deserted. Two men dressed in battered-looking tunics were standing a few paces away, smiling down at him. "Sorry, did thou say something?"

"Thou look lost."

"No, I'm not."

"Thou have lost something," the taller said.

"Thou are empty," the shorter man added. "Thou do not know the completeness which thou could feel. Thou could be filled with joyous life as ye carry the Blessed Children into being."

"Thou could know the embrace of the Mother."

"And ye would know peace and fulfillment at last."

A grimace twisted Geoff's face at their words. "Thou deluded fools!" he snarled. "Have ye encountered any of thy so-called *Blessed Children*?" he demanded. "Have thou looked at the true face of thy Mother?"

The men smiled vacuously at him.

Geoff stood up and hastily backed away from the pair, clutching his staff in his hand. "Thou are both mad. Leave me alone and never return."

"But we can feel thy emptiness."

"We can feel thy sense of loss."

"I lost my master to thy Mother's embrace!" Geoff snarled. "I will not lose myself."

A black-haired woman approached them, stepping out from behind a large stand of flowering lilacs. "Will he join us, Jacques?" The hem of her dress was ragged and dirty, but her face was clean.

"He is lost." The tall man shook his head sadly. "Worse, he refuses to even admit that he lost, nor will he accept direction onto the path to holiness."

Geoff's eyes narrowed as the woman drew closer. "Cynthia?"

The woman blinked at him, then recognition slowly dawned on her face. "Geoff?" she murmured.

"Cynthia, what are thou doing here?" He shook his head in confusion at her appearance. "I thought thou were dead. I mean, thou were in Conrad's tower after the storm and—"

"I was never in any danger." She smiled fondly at him. "No danger at all." She reached out her right hand towards him. "But thou are in pain, a soul in torment. Thou need to be found and helped, Geoff. There is no need for thee to remain lost."

He shook his head. "What happened to you?"

"I found the love of the Mother."

"We all found love," Jacques said.

Geoff took another step back, feeling his back press against the cold stone basin of the fountain. "Stay away from me!" he warned as he raised his ash staff. "Thou know that I am a mage!"

Cynthia laughed at that, a brittle sound verging on madness. "Thou were a bumbling apprentice, Geoff." Her expression hardened along with her voice. "Jacques, bring him. He will bow before the Mother and serve her will."

Geoff felt his staff being pulled from his hand. "Let go of me!" he protested. "Let go!"

* * *

"We subdued one group, but I'm certain other covens remain." Gavin's armour was dented and his moss green cloak had a tear in it. His sword was sheathed at his waist and he rested on hand on the hilt as he made his report.

Carolinka eyed him carefully. "Thou took prisoners?" The other courtiers were listening intently, as they were both aware. Priests and mages and city officials alike were growing ever more concerned by the growing disturbances as the cultists grew ever more bold.

"Yes. We are questioning them now."

"Hoping to uncover other covens?"

"Yes, my Lady." Josem offered her a nod of his head, the bells woven into his beard jingling softly. "They are not easily swayed into answering true questions. They preach their rhetoric endlessly."

"They resisted?"

"Aye, but not with lethal force." Gavin allowed a note of puzzlement into his voice. "Even when the battle was quite obviously lost, they still tried to subdue my men, not kill them. There are bruises and cuts aplenty, but few broken bones and no deaths. Thanks be to the Gods."

"Far be it from me to question such good fortune for my loyal guardsmen," the Baroness said, "but I like this not." She shook her head grimly.

"They want *converts*," Josem explained in a sour tone. "More hosts for their damned Mother."

"I will not allow their covens to remain at large. Gavin, use whatever troops thou deem necessary and subdue this erstwhile rebellion."

"As thou command, Baroness." He paused a moment, and licked at his lips. "And what of the planned expedition to Conrad's tower?"

"My heart tells me that such a journey might have to be delayed." Carolinka grimaced. "Yet it cannot be, for that is the apparent heart of this infection."

"I will lead what troops I can spare to journey north." Now it was Gavin who grimaced. "Fewer than I would like, given the need to keep civic order." He would not march from the city and leave the cultists a free hand to continue their riots and kidnappings.

"I expect no less from thee. Josem, I expect the priesthood to support the Guard."

The red and orange-robed priest nodded. "Our Protectors have fanned throughout the city seeking covens and nests of darkness. They will not fail to turn up traitors for due punishment." He turned his head towards another knot of courtiers. "So far the neighbourhoods near the College remain oddly quiet."

"The cultists know better than to challenge us," Pavel commented in a dry tone. He was holding his carved staff lightly in his right hand.

"And what have thee done to help safeguard the city?" Josem asked in a pointed tone. "Surely thou are doing something to help? It *was* a mage who began all of this trouble after all."

"I do not wish to see mages blasting the streets of my city with fire and lightning!" Carolinka snapped. "Matters are grave enough without such theatrics added to the mixture."

"Although we choose not to intervene in the quelling of riots, we do have a gesture of support to offer," the blue-robed mage announced with a glare for the priest. "We shall place potent enchantments onto the weapons of thy soldiers. They will be able to fight the Chthonians without fear that their acidic-blood will devour their swords and spears."

"A small favour," Josem replied.

"A useful favour." The Baroness nodded. "Thank you, Pavel."

"We can only cast a limited number of such enchantments," he warned her. "The spells are difficult to master and extremely draining for us to cast. Do not expect to have all of thy armies so equipped."

"Cast what spells thou can. I will be content." She had no other choice left to her, after all.

"We are offering up many prayers for the safety of thy soldiers, Baroness. People are flocking to the Temple to offer their prayers for victory over the demons."

"And the riots?"

"They have calmed somewhat." Gavin kept his voice steady. "Or burned themselves out. I fear that most of the Cultists have fled into hiding. Their continued attempts at preaching have only inflamed the populace against them. It will take time for them to regroup and rebuild their strength."

"Then this is a good thing." Josem smiled. "The common folk have learned to distinguish the lies of the Cult from the true faith of the Gods."

"For now I will be content with peace in my city. Ere the continuing disturbances bring out adventuresome neighbours seeking to aid us in quelling the riots." Carolinka kept her voice calm. She reached for a jewelled goblet held by a servant. "But where do these *dreams* come from? Is there some demon nesting within my city?"

"We have found no trace," Gavin told her. "No one has reported seeing any monsters roaming the streets. It would be difficult to dismiss a Cthonian once seen."

"Thanks be to the Gods!"

"We have sensed no magical rituals," Pavel said when Carolinka looked at him. "Aside from those within our College and the Temple that is."

"Tell me at once if thou hear otherwise. Gavin, double thy patrols. Any loosened demon must be found before it can cause harm."

"Of course, my Lady." He offered her a bow.

Chapter Fourteen

Geoff stepped from the final creaking wooden step onto the packed dirt floor of the basement, followed by a dozen raggedly-dressed cultists. He tried to pull free as Cynthia rested her hand on his arm, but other cultists held him too tightly.

The cellar was damp and barren, save for an oval urn resting on a brass stand atop a small table with. Torches crackled on the walls, sending shadows dancing on the walls and floors.

"Thou have been found at a most important time, Geoff." Cynthia turned away from him to gaze longingly at the urn. "Though the heretics and deluded followers of the false gods strive to subdue us, they will fail. Our victory is assured."

"Ordained?"

"Conrad was on the verge of greatness." She turned back to face him, a serene smile on her face. "He failed to grasp it."

"He died."

"He touched the moment of creation and paid the price," Cynthia said calmly. She ignored the other cultists who were continuing to gather in the cellar.

"He failed to find love." Jacques had locked the door and now approached them.

"He failed to embrace the Mother," a woman said. Her black hair was matted and tangled.

Geoff felt himself pushed closer to the altar.

A man dressed in a tunic and breeches of a very fine weave of cloth nodded. "Soon we shall be rewarded." He would not have looked out of place in the baroness's court. "Soon the Mother will bless us."

Geoff realized that what he had thought was an urn was actually leathery in texture, not pottery. "An egg," he whispered. "Ye Gods, 'tis an egg."

"Aye, a physical gift from the Mother."

"Tonight one of us will join with her...be filled with the wondrous life that she brings." Cynthia turned her head to look at Geoff with a joyful expression. "Perhaps it will even be thee."

Geoff tried to moisten his dry lips.

"Though the others have hunted us and our numbers dwindle, the faithful will again multiply. We will be fruitful and our blessed children will inherit the world."

The egg shivered.

Geoff tried to back away from the table, but the men holding his arms kept their grips tight.

"The birthing time draws near!" With fevered eyes, Cynthia pulled her blouse open. "The time of communion is upon us!"

"Union!" the others chanted.

Geoff shook his head. "What are you—?" he stared at the now-naked body of Cynthia. "I mean," he looked away and realized that everyone else was hastily stripping off his or her clothing.

"We must ready ourselves for communion."

"We must prove ourselves worthy." Jacques reached for Geoff's belt.

"Leave me alone!" the mage snapped.

"There is nothing to fear."

"Thou will commune with us." Cynthia leaned in close to his ear. "During our communion, *someone* will be embraced by the Mother."

"No, I cannot." Geoff shook his head. "Let me go!" His robes were being pulled away from his body, but he was unable to do more than struggle given the number of hands playing across his body. "Stop that!"

The torches seemed to flare more brightly.

"Communion!" Jacques turned to kiss one of his companions.

The egg shivered again.

Geoff felt himself pulled to the cold floor by the weight of many people.

The surface of the egg split open, like some obscene flower opening on a spring morning.

"No!" Geoff struggled, but he was pulled down into tangle of bodies. "No!" Someone was kissing him, many sets of hands roaming across his body.

Something black and skeletal scuttled across the table.

"Union!" someone screamed.

Icy fingers brushed across Geoff's leg.

"Union!" another voice cried out.

"Mmmm." Warm feelings swelled through Geoff's mind. *Love. Warmth.* "No!" A hand was at his throat. *Surrender.* Something cold pressed against his lips. "No!" Geoff screamed and the world seemed to explode.

* * *

Thunder boomed and the tavern seemed to shake.

"Odd," Norvgan said as he lifted a mug of ale to his lips. "It did not look like rain."

"These are distractions." Mikel slammed his fist onto the worn and scarred tabletop. "Distractions!"

The Dwarf nodded. "Aye, that they are."

"The cult keeps us occupied here in the capitol while their fellows spread their evil through the land."

"We have heard little from our scouts," Gavin countered.

Mikel poured himself more ale from the jug. "Little from the scouts, less from the priests." He drained his mug. "And nothing from the thrice-damned mages."

"I have received no word from my kin either," Norvgan admitted. "I sent messengers riding from Beaudral after Geoff cleansed that nest. The continued silence from the mountains worries me."

"Ye spoke of Goblin raids...mayhap they waylaid thy messenger."

"Or ate my dove?" The Dwarf grunted. "I suppose 'tis possible. Be content, Mikel, that for now thy city is at peace."

"Barely."

"My patrols are keeping the streets safe."

Mikel looked over at Gavin. "Thy patrols would be better used in the field laying siege to the mage's tower."

"Truth." Gavin nodded in agreement. "We will be leaving soon for that tower. A hard ride and a difficult task."

"Have ye asked the College for aid?"

Mikel did not answer.

Norvgan frowned and opened his mouth to repeat himself.

"Aye, we did but to no avail." Gavin shook his head. "Pavel has refused to send mages against another mage without good reason."

"Good reason?" Mikel demanded, his voice cutting through the noise of the tavern. "Good reason? We have proof that Conrad has unleashed a nest of demons into our midst and what help do the rest of them offer us? None!"

"Geoff is conducting—"

"Reading scrolls. Muttering over an orb. Bah!" He drained another mug and gestured to a serving maid. "No help at all."

Norvgan drained his own mug as Gavin shrugged.

* * *

"Now is the time for us to rise."

"To supplant the influence of the mages over the Baroness?" Josem could hear prayers being sung in the main Temple, but he had eyes solely for the Revered One. "This is our chance, a sign from the Gods that the continued reliance upon soulless magic is wrong." He lowered his voice. "We cannot spurn this gift."

"You call this a gift?" the elderly priest asked.

"A time of tribulation and suffering is good...it gives the flock purpose and visible proof of the need for their devotion." The temple coffers were filled with alms and tithes from parishioners and terrified citizens.

"Josem, we have sent many of our Wardens out of the city. The reports which have come back to us have been few and limited."

"Too much of the north remains infected with pockets of demonic influence and corruption. They must be lanced and healed."

The bells in the Temple towers tolled in their deep and sonorous way.

"Conrad's Tower must be razed."

"That is the plan set forth by the Baroness and her advisors...despite the objections of the College."

"I saw little evidence that the College was going to take direct action against their wayward colleague."

"Mayhap we should send Wardens to aide Count Grelfhaven."

The Revered One frowned. "Mayhap we should." He studied the other priest with narrowed eyes. "When does he ride forth?"

Josem lowered his head, the bells woven into his beard tinkling softly. "One day hence."

"With what strength?"

"A troop of men-at-arms. A hundred horsemen perhaps. And the Dwarf, of course."

"And how many mages?"

"The College refuses to take sides publicly." Josem did not bother to mask the scorn in his voice. "Arch-Mage Pavel claims to be conducting his own plan to deal with Conrad and his nest of demons."

"But not by sending aid with the Count?"

"Nay, Revered One."

The elderly priest grimaced. "Find me Wardens then, who are willing to march with Count Grelfhaven and Banner-Captain Gavin."

"As ye desire."

"I shall be in the atrium." The Revered One turned towards the main hall. "I wish to join the faithful in prayer for a time."

Josem bowed again.

Chapter Fifteen

Mikel was saddling his horse. The stallion looked at him and flared its nostrils. "We ride north!" he called out to the men also readying their mounts in the stable yard. "Let all who venture forth know the perils to be faced. Let any who do not feel themselves equal to this task admit as much and remain behind with no stigma."

None of the men broke ranks.

Mikel smiled.

"They're good lads," Norvgan said from where he stood next to a stallion. "Not as good as a band of Dwarfs, mind ye, but they have iron in their backbones." He was wearing a mail coat and wore a conical helmet atop his head. His beard hung down past his waist. "Be a good fight." He eyed the horse and grimaced. "A good time to have a stout Dwarf at thy side."

"'Tis always good to have a stout Dwarf and his axe at one's side," Gavin commented as he rode up. His cloak flapped in the stiff breeze, which he ignored as he carefully studied the men mounting up. "As opposed to having a Dwarf and his axe coming at ye."

Norvgan chuckled.

Half a dozen grim-faced men rode into the courtyard, all mounted on dark brown horses. They wore orange coats under their breastplates, with golden stripes on their orange breeches. They carried spears and had swords belted at their waists.

"Wardens," Gavin commented in a low tone. "A gift from the Revered One."

Mikel eyed them. "I knew nothing of this."

"Josem sought an audience last night to offer up this gift. He wished he could spare more, but many of their Wardens are already travelling through the northern farms and villages seeking out 'dens of corruption.'"

"I'll take whatever aid I can get," Mikel said as he eyed the wardens, "from honest men. These men will not falter easily when confronted by demons."

"The fight is to the north." Carolinka strode into the courtyard, with two armoured men-at-arms following her. She wore a black gown, with a jewelled dagger on her silver belt. Her gaze passed over the assembled soldiers, lingering for just a moment on the Wardens. "The Tower of Conrad is the centre of this evil. Thou must purge it from my barony."

"Then we ride north." Mikel climbed into his saddle. "Mount!" he called and the last of his men finished climbed into their saddles.

"I will ride with you."

"Thou?" Mikel stared at the speaker with cold eyes. The rest of the courtyard was suddenly silent as men watched the exchange.

Geoff looked shaken. There were dark circles under his eyes, matching the haunted look on his face, but he pressed on. "Thou need allies," he said. He had discarded his usual robes for a long green tunic and loose brown breeches, with a dark grey cloak draped about his shoulders. He finished riding his mount through the gateway and into the courtyard.

"I have an army already."

The Wardens all glared at the mage.

Geoff licked his lips. "Thou face creatures of magic."

"And thou claim that I need magic to fight against them?" Mikel's scorn was strong. "Thou are useless to me."

"I have my staff. I have powers."

"Ha!"

The Wardens continued to coldly watch and several rested their hands on the swords waiting in their sheathes.

"He speaks truth, Mikel," Norvgan stomped towards them. He had not yet mounted his horse. "How many of thy fellows will stand at thy side when confronted by such beasts as these Chthonians? How many will fight and how many of them will break and flee?"

"They will not break."

"Do not judge them until they have faced these demons in battle. We do not ride forth to face down brigands or rebels, nor Goblins, nor even natural dragons. This enemy be not one easily faced."

"They will not break."

"Fine, lad." Norvgan snorted. "The mage has faced these Chthonians before. Ye know that he will stand his ground now."

Mikel said nothing.

Carolinka merely watched.

The Dwarf snorted. "We know not what magical arts protect the Tower. Demons alone will be a challenge, but what traps might Conrad have woven to protect his home? Did ye think of such a risk? A mage might be vital to our success."

"And our lives," Gavin muttered.

"There be no other mages offered by the College. Accept what aid is offered to thee and be thankful."

Still Mikel said nothing.

"He comes," the Dwarf rested his weight upon his axe, "or *I* stay."

Carolinka's eyes widened.

"Fine! I suppose that he can ride with us." Mikel grimaced and spat into the dust. "But he rides as thy guest, Norvgan." He glared at Geoff, who looked startled. "But be warned! Betray me, Mage, and my blade will strike thou down ere thou can flee."

Geoff nodded. "I understand."

"My Lady Baroness, we ride." Mikel offered Carolinka a shallow bow, then flicked his reins. "We ride!"

Geoff gave his head a shake, then followed the column of riders out of the courtyard.

* * *

The column made good time once it had ridden beyond the city walls and out into the countryside.

Gavin had picked the best of his Guards and mounted them all on horseback. "Demons or no demons, I have a hundred knights and fifty archers," he boasted. "We can gather more from our patrols as we pass them by."

"The more men we take, the more victims we can offer the demons." Geoff kept his voice low.

"Don't worry, lad." Norvgan smiled at him. They were riding well back in the column, staying clear of Mikel and the Wardens. "If those Chthonians overrun us, I'll be sure to make certain thy head is freed from thy body ere I die." He patted the blade of his axe.

Geoff's face paled behind his beard.

Norvgan chuckled, then clutched at his reins. "Thrice-damned horse," he muttered.

Gavin rode closer to them. His eyes never stopped scanning the forest and farms they were travelling through. "The feelings of my comrade aside, I wish that we had more mages to aid us."

"I am still surprised that the College would not support thee."

"No doubt Arch-Mage Pavel knows more about this threat than we do," Gavin said in response. "He knows that we face an outbreak of Chthonians. He knows what happened to the Nostronomun Empire when they were overrun. So where is he now?"

Geoff shook his head. "I do not know the mind of the Arch-Mage nor the thoughts of the Conclave. I cannot presume to speak for them."

"Mikel was right. Thou are not much use to us then." He spurred his horse into a faster canter.

Geoff shook his head. "I do not know where the others are," he said to no one.

The Wardens twisted their heads to glare at him from where they rode.

"Ye cannot worry." Norvgan spat into the dust. "Anymore than I must like riding this damnable horse."

* * *

The column wound along the road with banners flying. The pine trees were thick and lush, limiting vision. Hooves thundered on the hard-packed earth as the horses galloped for a bit, then walked.

"'Tis was the best way for them to cover ground quickly, while not wearying the horses too badly."

"And the men?"

"Aye, we will need all of our strength to fight." Mikel kept a loose grip on his reins. "Battle might come upon us at any moment."

"Truth." Gavin had sent scouts ahead of the column, but the trees were thick enough to hide an army if it wished to remain hidden.

Mikel looked over his shoulder. "Can't thou cast some spell to track our foes?"

Geoff shook his head. "I have a scrying orb, but I can't use it while riding a horse."

"Why not?" Gavin demanded.

"Because it requires concentration. Staying in the saddle of this animal is hardly conducive to the proper frame of mind." Geoff spoke with an attempt at a mage's general disdain for non-magic users. "I will consult the orb when we stop for the night."

"Perhaps I don't plan to stop," Gavin replied with a grin. "A trained soldier can sleep in the saddle."

Geoff's eyes widened at that. "But I'm not a trained soldier," he said in alarm. "I can't sleep in the saddle of this damned beast!"

"Neither can I," Norvgan added. "Bad enough that I've got to ride this thing. There be no way I shall sleep on one. Feet on the ground. That's the proper place for a Dwarf."

"Ye ride well enough," Gavin pointed out.

"I need to cleave the heads from my foes, not trim their hair!"

"Don't discount the success of a trained mounted charge."

"Aye, lad, but neither should ye discount the effectiveness of a Dwarf with his feet resting firmly on rock! I will not sleep in the saddle."

"Thou can learn." Gavin laughed at their dismayed expressions. "Or thou can hope that I do call a halt for the night."

Norvgan snorted. "We have to stop...not even a Manling would be fool enough to ride through the night. Not when he knows that his foe can see plainly in the dark."

"And Mikel is no fool. He will seek every advantage he can."

"Aye, that he will."

* * *

The pine forest was dark.

No moon shone in the cloudless sky and even the stars seemed faint and shrouded.

Geoff looked around. "Where is everyone?" he asked aloud. Where had the camp gone? "Hello?"

The forest was so dark and quiet.

"Norvgan?"

Something hissed in the shadows.

"Stay away from me!" Geoff raised his empty hand and gaped at it. "My staff? Where is my staff?"

The bushes rustled.

"But there's no wind."

Another hiss sounded, this time from behind him.

Geoff's nerve broke and he ran.

Something clawed at his arm and he screamed...and tripped over a branch and found himself sprawled on the ground.

"Blasted fool!"

"Norvgan?" His heart was pounding. "Norvgan, the camp is gone and something—"

"What thing?" The Dwarf blinked at him.

Geoff looked around. A few watch fires were burning, showing men wrapped in their cloaks and blankets, while others stood guard. A horse neighed. "The camp."

"Aye, 'tis the camp." Norvgan slapped him on the arm. "Next time ye decide to go sleepwalking, walk the other way." He rolled himself back in his cloak. "Damned fool, mage." He began snoring almost immediately.

Chapter Sixteen

"There lies my master's tower." Geoff raised a trembling hand. He had dark bags under his eyes from the latest in a string of restless nights.

"Would that I had more men," Gavin muttered as he gazed across the low valley. He rested his hand on his sword.

"We have what we have and it will have to be enough." Mikel eyed the tower with a grim expression. "It's not very tall."

"'Twas tall enough for Conrad."

They were standing on a low rise, peering down into the valley and the structure in its heart. The tower was rather squat, holding maybe four levels, though it looked wide enough to hold numerous rooms on every floor. A low stone wall surrounded a modest courtyard and the tower itself was located in the centre. Black marks streaked the stones along the walls.

"As if fire tried to consume the place."

"A failed siege?" Gavin asked.

"My master is a mage...who would attack him?" Geoff shrugged, but as the others looked at him, he nodded. "The odd tribe of Goblins or a band of especially stupid bandits did try once or twice. A few fireballs or lightning bolts and they would flee."

"Always good to leave a few survivors," Norvgan agreed. "Need someone to pass the story along to other would-be raiders."

"Aye, that was Conrad's reckoning." Geoff gripped his staff more tightly. "Has it come to this?" he muttered.

"So, do we just walk in through the front door?"

"There is only the one door in the Tower."

"Wonderful."

"The village of Mardelis stands a few leagues to the west." Geoff gestured. "It is the closest village to the tower. 'Too close yet,' Conrad would often say. We can rest there tonight."

Mikel had already ridden a few steps down the hard-packed dirt road. He reined in his horse and looked back. "Why not ride forth and strike the tower now?"

Geoff shook his head. "Because the night is coming. I would rather not face these Chthonians in battle at night." *'Tis bad enough to face them by daylight.*

"The lad's right." Norvgan nodded, as did Gavin.

Mikel nodded reluctantly, resting his hand on his sword as he stared towards the tower. "Battles fought by day *are* easier," he finally said.

"On both sides."

"From all evidence," Gavin pointed out, "these creatures prey by night. They have the advantage to us in that."

"Ambush and slaughter is all well and good," Norvgan pointed out, "when ye be the one doing the ambushing. We venture down into yonder woods and I fear the ambush would be sprung upon us."

"Aye, I cannot argue with thy logic," Mikel said. "Damn it. Geoff, lead us to this village thou know."

"This way." The mage gestured.

* * *

"The village appears deserted."

"Aye, that it does." Norvgan sniffed the air.

The column rode forward, every man carefully studying bushes and trees and the houses as they approached.

There was an air of abandonment to the place. Houses were falling into disrepair and flowerbeds and gardens were choked with weeds.

"It has been abandoned for some time by the looks of those gardens." Geoff twisted his head around. "I like this not."

"Are there no priests nor patrols here?"

"There be no one here."

"The Dwarf speaks truth." Gavin reined in his horse. "What foul treachery has wrought this?"

Mikel surveyed the village. "We are close to the tower. No doubt the demons preyed upon the inhabitants early in the infestation."

A few pine trees stood here and there amongst the houses, but the forest had been cleared back for fields.

"Dismount!" Gavin called out. "Hobble the horses and search the village. No one travels alone!" he added hastily. "We know not what dangers might lurk within."

The men obeyed.

"No one travels alone." Norvgan nodded his approval as the men-at-arms began their search. "I see them going in squads." Five to ten men at a time were entering various houses.

The wardens entered the village's modest shrine. The orange sleeves of their coats stood out, even at a distance. They carried their spears ready for use, and looked ready to draw their swords in an instant.

Mikel nodded in approval. "Good fighters. I can tell they've seen action before."

A horseman was approaching the village at a gallop from along the south road. He reined in his steed and peered at the new arrivals. "Banner-Captain?"

"Guardsman, approach." Gavin waved him closer. His banner snapped in the wind as a trooper held it. "Do you have a report to offer?"

"Captain, thanks be to the Gods!"

Gavin's eyes narrowed at the obvious relief in the man's voice. "What happened?"

"Creatures in the night." The man was pale and there was dried blood on his breastplate. He slid from his saddle and landed heavily on the ground. "We rode into Mardelis some two nights back. A dozen of us, under Bannerman Jessup. The village was deserted, or so we thought. We rode our first patrols through the rest of the valley, and then last night we settled in."

"And thou were attacked?" Mikel had approached, followed by Geoff and Norvgan.

"'Twas near dusk when a villager staggered out of the forest babbling loudly about monsters. 'Terrible dragons' she called them. She was mad. We had to restrain her in a room at the inn." He shuddered at the memory. "'Twas just after midnight when she screamed loud enough to wake the dead."

Mikel eyed him.

"She began screaming that the Mother was near and that she was going to give birth to the Mother's children. Then she shrieked in pure agony."

"Go on," Gavin prompted after a moment.

The guardsman shook his head. "It was a terrible sound. Screaming as if she was going deafen us all. Thought I was going to go mad.

"Then Colin cried out. He was guarding the horses. When we got there, our horses were galloping about loose...some of them. Colin was gone...just his spear laying on the ground."

Murmurs came from the men who had gathered to listen.

"Silence!" Mikel ordered. "What about the rest of thy squad?"

"Even as we stood gaping at the horses, and called for Colin, the demons came for us. Dozens of them erupted from within the trees. Bluish-green bodies glinting in the moonlight, mouths filled with fangs, they were unstoppable." He was shaking now. "They just kept coming and killing...."

Gavin frowned. "Ye Gods." He closed his eyes. "Ye Gods," he repeated in a soft voice.

"We must seek out a place of shelter. It will be night soon." Geoff looked up at the westering sun. "We can barricade ourselves in the houses."

"They broke through the doors! They broke in and took everyone! *Everyone*!"

"Guardsman!"

The man stiffened at Mikel's shout and fell silent.

"What is thy name?"

"Oscar, Sir."

Mikel tried to make his voice soothing. "Oscar, we know about these demons. I have faced them several times in battle and I have slain them. The Dwarf has as well."

Geoff said nothing.

"They do not frighten us," Mikel continued. He hoped the rest of the patrol was listening and taking heart from his words. "We know that they will come and we will be waiting for them. It will not be a slaughter of men tonight, but a rather a slaughter done by men!"

Oscar swallowed, but he looked calmer.

"What's the strongest building?"

"The inn." One of the Wardens spoke up. "Few windows and 'tis large enough to hold us all." He gestured at it with his spear.

"Then we will make our stand there. Stable the horses round the back and double the guards."

"Triple the guards," Gavin countered. He paused, but Mikel said nothing. "Short watches, with weapons at hand."

The Dwarf nodded. "They will come for us." He stroked the blade of his axe with his thumb. "I will be waiting."

"Prepare a meal," Gavin ordered one of his sub-captains. "I suspect that having a cook fire or two will make little difference in attracting them."

"We had no cook fires, Banner-Captain, yet still they came."

"They might have been hunting that woman."

"Or they might be watching the roads for travellers. Who can know the mind of a demon?" Gavin frowned. "Send troops for a quick ride through the closest forest, but tell them to be back before nightfall."

"Aye, these beasties come mostly at night."

Several men hurried to their horses.

Geoff drew a crystal sphere from his pouch and rubbed it with his sleeve. "Yes, we should hurry." He peered into its depths, narrowing his eyes. "There is a storm coming. I can sense it."

"Rain?" Gavin looked up at the sky. "That will play havoc with our bowstrings."

"Not that kind of storm...'tis a gathering, no more like a swirling in the air. It is not something easily explained."

Mikel snorted and Geoff recoiled. "Fine, I'll leave thou to worry about it then. I must make plans for things of flesh and blood that I can kill." He stalked towards the inn, calling for men to barricade the windows and the door.

Norvgan snorted, blowing out his black beard. "The lad pushes himself too hard. 'Tis not a good thing."

"He carries much guilt," Gavin reminded him. "Much guilt," he repeated, giving Geoff's back a look as well.

Chapter Seventeen

Flat-topped towers rose towards the heavens, their white marble stones gleaming in the light cast by the setting sun.

Geoff looked around. The sprawling city appeared peaceful under the coming twilight. Red-trimmed banners flapped in the wind, the red hawks on them seeming to fly against a blue false-sky.

He looked upwards again as the sun finished setting in a fiery blaze. The stars were moving.

Geoff stared as dozens of stars flared brightly against the black sky. The stars grew larger and began leaving trails of fire as they arced across the sky and vanished beyond the horizon.

And then the ground shook under his feet.

* * *

The full moon was bright, nearly blinding as Geoff opened his eyes and sat up with a yawn. "Ye Gods," he muttered. "Such a dream I just had."

Norvgan was sitting near an unshuttered window, smoking his pipe. His axe rested on the floor beside him.

"Did thou dream?" the mage asked in a tired voice. He could hear men snoring from where they lay wrapped in their blankets. The upper floors of the inn were all occupied by sleepers.

"I don't dream."

"Lucky you."

Norvgan snorted. "I don't dream of the Mother or of monsters. I was dreaming of proper Dwarf things. Mountains of gold. Axes hewing the necks of my foes." He gripped his beard and gave it a tug. "Proper things. Thy fellow Manlings are the ones muttering about the Mother."

"What was that?"

Norvgan shrugged. "I slept and then awoke to take my turn at watch. A good dozen of thy fellows are muttering about the Mother even now."

Geoff paled. "That is not good." He stood up, feeling his back creak softly. "Ye Gods, that is not good." He hurried to the side of one man rolled in his cloak and knelt down. "Mikel?"

Mikel's brown eyes opened in an instant and his hand had already seized the hilt of his sword. "What do thou wish, Mage?" he growled.

"Men are dreaming about the Mother. Were you?"

Mikel sat up. "No." He looked around the dark room. "Thou woke me up for that?"

"The dreams herald an attack. I thought thou should be awakened before it begins." Geoff straightened. "I sense something." He returned to where he had been sleeping and quickly picked up his staff. "I think the demons are close."

"Thy master's tower—"

"Is their nest. They will hunt for prey...and right now, we are likely the largest group of potential prey around."

"There's movement in the fields," Norvgan announced calmly from the window. "Lots of shadows."

"Damn it." Mikel stood up. "If this is some joke—"

"To arms!" a voice cried out. "Attack from the south!"

"The south?"

"They flanked us."

The inn stood at the centre of the small village. There was a large square between it and the rest of town's buildings.

Gavin stood in the square with sword and shield held ready. "To arms!" he bellowed for the fourth time.

Guardsmen were hurrying to join him in the square, taking up ranks and readying their weapons.

"Light those torches! We need light!"

Several guardsmen hurried to obey.

Mikel hurried out of the inn. "The south?" His dark blue cloak flapped in the night breeze.

"Aye."

Torches attached to buildings flared as men hastily kindled them.

Screams echoed in the night.

Gavin's eyes narrowed. "Damn it! The scouts are not able to disengage and fall back to us."

Mikel shook his head, but he was still studying the street. "This foe cannot fly, nor breath fire. We can make our stand here and see them coming."

"True enough."

Gavin gestured towards one of streets from which the sounds of dying men could still be heard. "Archers, ready!"

"Terrible time for a battle." Norvgan stomped to their side as the archers formed a skirmish line behind other men holding spears and shields. "Just getting ready to go back to sleep. Didn't even have time enough to finish my pipe."

"We can try to keep the noise down while you slumber," Gavin told him.

Norvgan smiled and chuckled. "Nay, Manling. I'm awake now and could do with some exercise to tire myself ere I return to my blankets."

"Hopefully you will enjoy it." Gavin looked around. "Where's the mage?"

"Who cares?" Mikel replied.

Chthonians erupted from the night into the light cast by the torches. Their jaws gaped open as they hissed and their long tails lashed back and forth.

Murmurs came from the men.

"Steady!" Mikel ordered. "We're ready for them."

The Chthonians hissed again, and then they began to scuttle up the street at a brisk pace.

"Loose arrows!" Gavin watched as the first volley arced over his head.

Half a dozen demons fell with inhuman shrieks, but the others immediately clambered over the bodies of their fellows and kept coming.

A second volley of arrows sought out more victims.

"Ready swords." Gavin kept his voice calm, though he pitched his voice to carry through the night.

Mikel waved his own sword over his head. "Strike and then move aside. Never stop moving. Watch out for their blood—it burns worse than fire."

The Wardens drew their over-long swords and waited for the demons to close.

The ranks of men stood ready, shields in front and spears ready to stab.

"Keep them back," Mikel warned. "Strike and move."

Lightning flared from an upper-floor window of the inn and stabbed into a cluster of demons.

"I see the mage has not fully lost his nerve."

"Yet." Mikel held his sword ready. "But he's hiding."

Norvgan snorted. "He has chosen his place to die." He hefted his axe as the demons got closer and he smiled. "As have I." He charged, waving his axe overhead. "Geerraaaa!"

"Bloodthirsty little fellow." Gavin watched as the Dwarf chopped a demon in half with his axe and greenish blood splattered the street.

"Aye, that he is." Mikel offered up a quick prayer for the Dwarf.

More lightning flared from the window to lash the eastern street.

One Warden screamed as greenish-blue claws slashed through his breastplate. Even as he fell, two demons leapt over him to attack his comrades.

Screams rang out.

"The west flank!" Mikel shouted as he turned. "More of them!"

"Flankers." Gavin cursed loudly. "My spearmen are not holding."

"So many of them." They simply appeared out of the night to strike and kill before slipping back into the shadows. Mikel took a step towards the west as demon dropped from a rooftop to crush a man. "They need help."

"So does the east!"

"I can hold here!" Norvgan called. "Blood price!" he screamed as he hewed down another Chthonian.

Lightning lashed the street again.

Gavin lopped the head from one beast, then ducked as claws reached for his own head. "Steady men!" he shouted as he hurried west.

· Chapter Eighteen

"We lost half our men." Gavin sounded dejected.

"We lived through the night." Norvgan was carefully wiping his axe blade clean with a cloth. "Can't ask for more than that."

"Half of us are dead."

"Or missing." Geoff spoke up from the other side of the inn's common room. Parchments were scattered on the table in front of him. "At least half of the fallen cannot be found."

Gavin spat. "Taken away by those damned Chthonians."

"Aye, lad." Norvgan dropped the cloth onto the sawdust-strewn floor and watch it dissolve with a long hiss.

Mikel turned away from the window to look at his comrades. "But why?" he demanded. "They left their own fallen." After a moment, he turned back towards the window.

Men were slowly gathering the bodies, carefully dragging them to a freshly dug pit. The demonic blood seemed to lose some of its potency after death, though the wounds still bled. Other men stood guard, arrows knocked on their bows.

"They did not take dead bodies away with them...but only still-living prisoners." Geoff kept his voice steady.

Mikel spat. "Hosts."

The mage nodded, his expression grim.

"Ye merciful Gods." Gavin slumped down into a chair. "Ye Gods." His cloak was torn in half a dozen plates and his breastplate was scratched, but he was otherwise hale.

Norvgan tossed him a wineskin.

Gavin drank. "We haven't got the strength to assault the tower now."

"We can't remain here," Geoff said. "The Chthonians will almost certainly come back for another night raid. I do not think we can hold them off again."

"We should send the wounded back at least. Every man who can still ride can guard them."

"We have very few wounded," Gavin pointed out. "The battle did not leave many wounded and still breathing."

"Even the dead demons can still slay." Mikel watched the men-at-arms use long poles and hooks to drag the demons to the burial pit so they could avoid the acidic blood.

"We need a better strategy."

"Aye, lad, that we do."

Two Wardens marched past, glancing at the mage.

"We must destroy the nest. Conrad's tower."

Geoff looked at them. "But the army was beaten. We can't still mount an attack in force." He nearly dropped his staff.

Mikel paced towards him. "We must destroy the nest. That is why we came here."

Gavin nodded. "I have a few men still brave enough to venture there. A small party can still penetrate the tower."

"Thou are quite mad," Geoff protested.

"The tower belonged to a mage. There must be something stored in there—some chemicals or potions—that we can use to destroy the place."

"Black powder perhaps?"

"I've got black powder among our stores," Gavin reminded them. "We can use that."

"Madness! Those demons will rip thou apart long before thou can reach the tower's inner chambers." Geoff rose to his feet. "We must flee back to the city. We can plan anew and gather fresh allies to—"

"The city walls will not hold back the demons forever!" Mikel snarled. "And I will not flee in fear. We held last night. We will end this."

"The Chthonians will return tonight. They will come until there are none of us left alive."

"Then ye should flee back to the city and thy College. Mayhap Pavel will protect thee with some spell."

Geoff flinched.

"What spooks you?" Gavin demanded.

"Nothing."

"Something changed you." Norvgan snorted. "You're different to how thou were in the city. Something changed you."

"Nothing changed me." Geoff shook his head. "But ye are the ones acting foolishly."

"We simply do what we must."

* * *

The pine trees were rustling in the warm breeze.

Geoff held the crystal orb in his hand. "Damn it!" He threw the orb to the ground and watched it roll across the dirt.

"Is that some new form of spell casting?" Norvgan picked up the orb in his fist and stared into it. "A pretty enough jewel."

Geoff reached for the jewel. "And it is just a jewel to you." He slid it back into his belt pouch.

"Aye. We Dwarfs have little use for magic. Ye Manlings place far more faith in it and reliance upon it."

"Too much sometimes."

"So what happened back in the city?"

"Happened?"

The Dwarf nodded and took a step closer. "Aye, lad. One day yer Lord High Mage declares that no mage will march against Conrad's tower with the Baroness's army, and then thou show up to volunteer."

Geoff shook his head.

"Something happened."

"Nothing happened."

"Something did." Norvgan paused a moment. "Tell me or tell another, but thou must speak of it eventually."

Geoff took a few steps away.

Norvgan plopped himself down onto the ground. He took out his pipe and carefully began to fill the bowl.

"I met a woman." Geoff sighed aloud. "Cynthia was a servant in Conrad's tower. Same time I was there. The same time when Conrad made his experiments with the dragon eggs." He paused a moment. "She survived, somehow, and fled to the city."

"Survived?"

"She, she embraced the Mother."

"Ah." Norvgan puffed on his pipe.

"I had no idea she still lived. I thought that she was dead. Everyone else who had been in the tower was slain by the Chthonians when they burst forth from the cellars, so how was I to know differently?

"A few days back, ere we left the city, Cynthia encountered me in one of the gardens, with a group of fellow cultists, and they dragged me off to one of their foul covens. One of the last active ones in the city from what she told me."

"A coven eh? Did they try one of them fertility rites with ye?" Norvgan chuckled as the mage blushed. "Oh, they did!. Typical ploy," he finished with a snort. "No imagination in them."

"It wasn't just that. There were a good two or three dozen of them there. Maybe even more. It was rather hard to tell."

"Too many arms and legs?" The Dwarf laughed more loudly. "Too many other parts as well, eh lad?"

"They had a Chthonian egg."

Norvgan's laughter cut off abruptly. "Did they now?"

"They were blessed by the Mother with it. It was to be the centre of their coven. During the ritual, someone was going to be impregnated."

"Thee?"

"A...a demon tried. The incubus was nothing like the stories. No fair feminine creature of alluring and unearthly beauty." The mage shuddered, his eyes closed tight. "It was far from beautiful. Skeletal. Black. Spider-like. Too many legs. Gods!"

"Ye survived though."

"I burned it." Geoff whispered that part. His eyes were still closed.

"Good for ye."

"I burned it."

Norvgan sucked at his pipe. "Damn thing's gone out."

"I burned it. I burned them." Geoff's tone was conversational as his eyes opened. "I burned the house down."

"Thou blew the house *up*." Gavin stepped around the corner of the barn, followed by Mikel. "Thou destroyed it as if by lightning."

Geoff blinked and his mouth hung open.

"I was part of the patrol which happened upon the aftermath. I did not see thee there," he paused, "among the debris."

"Typical." Mikel was holding his drawn sword and glaring at the mage. "Thou do like thy lightning."

"I didn't mean to do it! I never meant too."

"So perhaps thou aren't totally useless."

"So will you ride to the tower with us?" Gavin asked.

After a moment, Geoff nodded.

Gavin clapped his hand down on Geoff's shoulder. "Good. Then there is hope of success for us."

Mikel turned to leave them. "Just don't go and destroy the tower with us inside it." He walked away.

· Chapter Nineteen

The pine trees were half-dead and the air smelled of rot. Geoff stared at the waiting tower. Everything was so quiet. The world was still, without any birds singing or even tree limbs moving with the breeze.

The gates in the wall were gaping open.

"Like the maw of a beast."

Geoff started. "Don't do that!" he snapped. His heart was already pounding in his chest and they had yet to even enter the courtyard.

Gavin smiled as the mage clutched at his chest. "Thou never heard us approach...what makes thee think thou would hear a demon?"

"I could've blasted thee."

"What are thou doing here?" Norvgan asked after the mage's protests had fallen silent.

"I was going inside." Geoff gestured. "A mage started this mess so a mage should go and clean it up. Conrad was my master..."

"Thou can't go in there alone." Gavin gestured. "I have a dozen men waiting to follow us." Most of his men had been left in the village, to guard the wounded and wait.

"They'll stand no chance."

"A group stands a better chance than one alone."

Mikel slipped to their sides, carrying a bared blade. "No sign of any demons around. They must all be inside."

"Great."

"They do seem to be far more active at night. We should be gone far from this place by then...unless thee know of some stronghold?"

"There are no strongholds within many leagues. Conrad valued his privacy."

"I thought as much." Gavin turned his head. "Kurt, Heinrich, carry those casks forward."

The two burly men picked up the casks from the ground and Geoff hurriedly brushed past them.

"Geoff, the black powder is dangerous."

"I am a mage. Mere chemicals do not frighten me." He straightened and brushed a stray leaf from his bronze-coloured tunic. "If we are going, then we should hurry."

"Got any useful spells to speed our journey?"

"Nothing that would be of help." Geoff licked his lips.

"Then we go." Mikel strode forward, his eyes twitched from side to side as he kept watch for attackers.

Geoff had taken the lead, striding forward with his ash staff held loosely in his right hand.

"Why are the pines half-dead?" Norvgan asked.

"I have no idea."

"Just asking. There seems to be no reason for it."

"They lived when Conrad lived. Now, they die." Geoff eyed the scorch marks on the stones of the tower. "Perhaps the heat which burned the tower did something to the trees."

"These are dying, not burned."

"I have no answers for thee, Mikel. Now keep silent and do not distract me with idle questions. Thy lives might depend upon my concentration." His grip tightened on his staff.

The gates hung open enough that the adventurers could enter the courtyard freely.

"Last chance to turn back." Geoff made the offer, but no one took him up on it.

The adventurers slipped through.

Gavin eyed the courtyard, as his two archers kept their bows ready. "Empty courtyard."

"Stables are over there." Geoff gestured to a thatch-roofed building. "There used to be horses and cattle there."

"I doubt any still live."

"Not given the demons breeding habits."

"Nor their likely need for food."

"Aye, there is that as well."

"How do we enter the tower?"

"The door is there." Geoff swallowed—his throat had gone quite dry. It had been torn from its hinges and splintered wood was scattered near the wall. "The cellar doors are at the end of the farthest hallway. After we go inside, take the first left, and look for a door."

"Thou heard him. Go."

"Keep thy swords to hand," Mikel ordered. "They might strike from ambush at any time."

The interior of the tower was bright.

The walls were bare stone, with no tapestry nor shelves.

"Why are the torches lit?"

"Conrad didn't like the dark." Geoff eyed one of the dragon-claw shaped sconces and nodded as he passed it by. "He wove an enchantment on them. They'll burn like that for years."

"The flame is cold." Norvgan eyed it. "Looks a bit blue."

"It's magical." Geoff shrugged. "It burns bright with no risk of fire. So thee will be unable to use it to ignite the black powder," he added.

Gavin nodded as he realized that fact.

"We'll rely on thy lightning for ignition." Mikel eyed the stone walls. They appeared to have been blackened by fire in places. "No display of riches?" he asked. "I expected treasures. Instruments and the other trappings of magical rituals." It was rather disappointing.

"Conrad did not believe in idle displays of wealth," Geoff explained. "Most mages keep their ritual implements in their studies and sanctums, not on display for passers-by and visitors to ogle."

"There is a smell to this place."

"Aye." The Dwarf wrinkled his nose. "Damp and rotting. Smells like a jungle."

"'Tis not magic." Geoff sniffed at the air, noting the out-of-place scent. "This is, no doubt, some aura of the demons we hunt."

"Reminds me of the smell in the watch tower."

"Aye, that it does." Mikel gestured forward with his sword. "The cellars, Mage."

Geoff pointed. "That way."

"Why do ye want the cellar? Why not seek the upper floors?"

"What better place for a demon to nest than underground?" Mikel countered. "Just like the farmhouse?"

"True enough." Geoff nodded slowly. "And because Conrad used the cellars for his first experiments. The Mother is likely below ground."

"We head below."

One of the guards cursed.

"What, Jaime?"

"The wall is slimy," the man replied with a sheepish grin as he wiped his hand on his breeches. "I didn't expect it to be." He had a scar on his cheek.

"Slimy?" Geoff hurried to check for himself. "Hm." He rubbed some of the thick clear gel between his thumb and forefinger, then wiped it on his cloak with a grimace.

Gavin frowned. "What is it?"

"Nothing of importance." Geoff looked around the corridor, cocking his head to listen. "We should hurry...I do not know how long those demons will sleep, if they do sleep, but we cannot risk discovery here."

"Aye, lead on."

Mikel glanced at the guardsmen. They looked nervous, but no man seemed about to break and abandon them. "Lead on."

Geoff reached for the door handle. "This way."

The stairs were lit by more the magical torches.

"The stairs stop often," Geoff explained as they stepped into a large room. "The gap between levels covers much area."

"Storeroom of some kind?" Mikel eyed the place. There were a number of tables scattered about, many of which had been overturned.

"Nay, 'twas a meeting room." Geoff eyed the doors that ringed the room. "The servants slept through there. The kitchen is through that door."

"It smells worse in here." The Dwarf wrinkled his nose. "The air is tainted with something foul and rotting."

"'Tis the food in the storerooms most likely."

"The kitchen is through there?"

"Aye, but I doubt we would fine much wholesome to eat."

"True," Gavin nodded. "Let us—"

The door burst open and demons issued forth in a tide of claws and fangs.

"Ambush!" Norvgan hurled himself at the Chthonians. His axe sliced through one's waist and greenish blood sprayed.

Gavin and Mikel raised their swords, as did the gaurdsmen.

Geoff stared, open-mouthed.

Acidic blood hissed on the stones and the air was tainted with foul-scented smoke.

"Another victory."

"Aye, another victory."

Geoff gave his head a shake. The ambush had been swift and brutal, but the guardsmen had slain their foes without losing a man. *And I did nothing to aid them,* he thought bitterly. *Not even a single lightning bolt.*

Norvgan stomped away from the now-doorless kitchen. "Nothing left to eat in there," he said, "at least not for the likes of us." He shuddered. He had cast aside his cloak.

"Should we check the servants' rooms?" Jaime asked. He was still breathing heavily after the short but vicious battle.

"I doubt there is any reason to bother." Geoff shook his head and leaned on his staff. "If any demons waited there, they would have attacked us with their kin." There would be no servants waiting.

Mikel checked his sword. *The enchantment seems to be working...no sign of damage from the Chthonians I've slain.*

"An evil thought takes me."

"Oh, Gavin?"

"Aye. If these demons are like inferno-spawned insects, then this must be their nest."

Geoff nodded his head. "A logical thought, thus far."

"And insects usually have a leader...a queen."

Mikel looked at his comrade with realization dawning in his eyes. "And insect queens are usually larger than their drones."

Gavin nodded.

"Ye Gods," Norvgan murmured. "The Blessed Mother."

Geoff eyed the demon corpses. "Another logical conclusion." He took a tighter grip on his staff. "But she can still die. We have proven that often enough."

"Or so we hope."

"Where are the stairs?"

"Through that doorway." Geoff pointed.

"What's on the walls?" Jaime asked.

Mikel tapped one with the blade of his sword. "Resin of some kind?" The looping coils looked brittle, yet felt solid enough.

"Just like back in the watch tower." Norvgan snorted. "Another sign of the demons."

"Nice of them to leave a calling card."

Another staircase led them deeper underground.

"It's getting dimmer."

"Impossible!" Geoff protested. "Conrad enchanted all of the torches in the tower. They will burn for years to come."

Gavin shook his head. "It *is* getting dimmer."

"He's right."

"The resin is covering the torches." Geoff bent his head so that he could study one more closely. "It does not burn, but it eats the light."

"So we could be fighting in pitch dark when we reach the bottom of these stairs?"

"Possibly," Geoff admitted to Mikel. "Though I hope not." He continued down the stairs.

The stairs ended in a large room with four doors.

"Storerooms behind those two," Geoff pointed. "Unused cell there."

"Check them all," Mikel ordered. "Jaime, take that one. Oscar, check the cell."

Geoff ignored the guardsmen as they obeyed the order. "That one has a tunnel leading further down."

"Further down?" Norvgan smiled broadly. "Finally, we're going to a decent place."

"How much farther down does this place go?"

"I-I'm not sure. I was seldom summoned into the lowest levels."

The air in the dim stairwell was growing damp.

"This Conrad must have been half-Dwarf." Norvgan rested his weight on his axe as he studied the resin on the walls. "We are already deeper than most Manlings go."

"And we'll go deeper yet. Down that tunnel." It curved downward, the walls and ceiling and stairs alike covered with coils of the odd resin.

"They spread their nest thoroughly."

"And they incorporate many materials." Gavin stepped over the skull of a cow.

"The air is growing ever more moist...'tis like wandering through the Mist Loch."

"They've covered the torches more thoroughly here."

"Interesting." Geoff looked more closely. The resinous material did cover the torch, like a cocoon, but the bluish light was still shining dimly through. He reached out to touch it, carefully, with his finger. "Not hot," he muttered. "Not even warm." He grimaced and turned to face the others. "We must be cautious as we approach the tunnel to the ritual chamber."

They descended still deeper and the stairs ended.

"So many tunnels." Geoff eyed them as the main tunnel spit in half a dozen directions. "I-I don't recall all of them being here."

"What do thou mean?"

"There should be just one tunnel. I have no memory of this chamber." He shook his head. "This makes little sense to me." The openings were rougher than those above. "The Chthonians must be digging new tunnels."

"Wonderful," Mikel snapped. "So we're lost then?"

"No..." Geoff shook his head. "I can sense a magical presence." His eyes were half-closed. "It lays close by."

Gavin looked at the mage. "Are ye still with us? Now is no time for sleeping."

"I'm not sleeping...it's a powerful presence."

Mikel snorted. "We should just lay out the black powder and ignite it." Two of the guardsmen nodded their agreement.

"Nay, that won't work. If we're not close enough to their nest, we'll not kill them all."

"We keep moving then. I will not settle for half-measures. We must be certain."

"Aye, Mikel, that we must."

· Chapter Twenty

Geoff was staring vacantly down the corridor, his lips moving silently.

The men-at-arms exchanged looks and muttered amongst themselves.

"What is it?" Gavin asked.

"'Tis the air."

"Aye, Captain."

"What of the air, Heinrich?"

The man pursed his lips, as if ready to spit. "The air stinks of burning and rot."

"Aye," Norvgan nodded. "It does."

Gavin grimaced. "I thought this place was fireproof?" He turned to the mage. "Geoff, you claimed there is no risk of fire here."

The mage slowly blinked his eyes, as if awakening from sleep. Finally, he nodded. "Aye. The torches cannot set the tower alight."

"You're hiding something."

Geoff turned his head towards Mikel. "No, I'm not."

Mikel pushed forward and pressed the flat edge of his bared sword to Geoff's throat. "Thou lie," he said coldly.

"No!"

"Thou lie!"

"No, I don't!"

Gavin shook his head.

"Mikel, leave him alone."

Norvgan pushed Mikel away from Geoff. "Easy there, lad."

Mikel shook his head. "That damned mage is holding something back. Something that could get us all killed."

"No, I'm not."

"Then why do we smell the stench of old burning? Why is the tower's exterior blackened? *What* are thou hiding?"

Geoff shook his head. "Nothing." He turned away, gesturing down the long tunnel. "We must keep moving. Just beyond this corridor is the—"

Part of the wall had been hollowed out in a room-sized chamber, its walls covered with the resinous chitin. The material was not laid down evenly and rough rock gaped through in patches, as did the exposed bones of beasts and of people.

"By the Gods!"

Mikel turned away from the sight. "Those are living people," he muttered. "Mage, what has thy master wrought?"

Geoff was also looking extremely shaken by the sight before them. "They were once, but they are not now." He gripped his staff more tightly.

Not all of the corpses had decayed. Several were still intact enough to be seen for what they were: people were cocooned into the very walls, their faces contorted into expressions of agony.

"Thou knew about this!" Gavin accused.

Geoff paled. "I was...aware of such a fate, yes."

One of the guardsmen staggered several paces away before being violently sick.

"Is this more of thy master's work?" Mikel demanded. His voice was cold, though his face was pale.

Geoff shook his head. "Conrad didn't sacrifice people...just cattle. And a few Goblins." The mage paled further. "By all the Gods, I swear he didn't use Humans or Dwarfs for this...perversion!" He gripped his staff with white-knuckled hands. "By all the Gods, I swear it."

"Is this what thou saw in the farmhouse cellar?" Norvgan asked. The Dwarf sounded calm, undisturbed by the horrific sight. He reached up to stroke his black beard.

The silence stretched out for a long moment.

"Aye."

"And the poison I've seen thee carrying in thy belt pouch? Was that something thou always carry with thee? Or is it just in case thou might be captured by these *things*."

Geoff swallowed.

"Or was it meant for us?" Gavin asked.

"No!" Geoff protested. "The poison was meant for me...should I be captured. I will not be used as a host for their breeding."

"Ye gods!" A cry rang out from Jaime.

Not all of the bodies cocooned into the wall were dead.

One of them was one of the Wardens who had gone missing from the camp. He was fastened to the wall by coils of dried resin at his wrists and legs. "Help me!" he gurgled, wide-eyed and gasping. Sweat was pouring down his white face. "Help me, Banner-Captain. Please."

Gavin nodded. "We'll cut him loose. Jaime—"

"Aye, allow me." Norvgan hefted his axe.

"It is too late for him." Geoff tapped what looked like a broken pottery jug with the toe of his boot. "He has been infected."

"We can cure him," Mikel said. "We'll find a real mage and...."

"He will not last the night." Geoff's tone was cold and harsh.

"Gods!" The Warden writhed and screamed. "Please, help me! The pain is...Gods!"

Gavin gripped his sword as the man cried out again. "We must do something."

"Aye, but there is but one choice."

"We can't let him suffer."

Gavin stared at him. "We can't just—"

"There is but one thing we can do for him." Geoff swallowed, then hardened his voice. "He must be killed."

There was a moment of silence.

"More poison?" Mikel hissed. "To ease him into eternal sleep?"

Geoff nodded.

"Poison is thy preferred means of dealing with the victims of thy mage-summoned disaster."

Geoff flinched.

"That was thy cure for Franz as well!"

Geoff recoiled.

"I hope that thou will taste thy own poison at some point."

"Do thou think that I enjoy this?" Geoff snarled. "Do thou truly believe that I wish to gaze upon the suffering of my fellows?" He flung his hand towards the gruesomely-adorned wall. "What kind of monster do thou take me for?"

Mikel looked abashed at the tirade.

Norvgan grunted. "We have little time for such discussion. Mikel, we have journeyed with Geoff enough now that ye must know his true heart."

"Aye," Mikel nodded as the Warden groaned again.

"I can feel it," the man grunted. "Sharp...in my chest."

"The demon is growing rapidly." Geoff removed the vial from his ouch. "I promise it grants a swift and painless sleep."

Mikel stared at the vial.

"It is the only way."

"He's right," the Warden gasped.

Norvgan looked at them. "Well?" He was still holding his axe, ready to swing. "One blow and I can ease his suffering."

"I can feel it, growing inside me."

Geoff stood silently.

"Please," the Warden's face was screwed up in pain. "Kill me!"

Gavin swallowed. "Do it," he whispered.

Mikel had hurried off along the corridor. He could no longer hear the Warden's pained gasps or cries. He couldn't hear the murmuring of his comrades either.

"That Gods damned mage!" he muttered. "The whole college has too long been reliant upon their spells. The priesthood have the right of it...sorcery is a foul taint and should be outlawed." *And yet*, a voice whispered in his thoughts, *what other weapons would avail thee against these foul magic-spawned demons?* Of course, Mikel countered to himself, had Conrad not experimented with the dragon eggs, then these demons would never have been spawned. *Or would they have still spawned and now infest the barony unstopped?*

It was hard to be certain.

Mikel kicked at a pebble and watched it bounce along the rough stone floor.

"Mikel?" Gavin called out in a low voice. "It can't be safe here. Thou should not wander far."

Mikel turned so that he could look back along the corridor. "I've not gone far," he said. "Merely a quick scout of the path ahead." He gestured with his sword. "No sign of demons."

The wall seemed to move.

"Chthonians!"

Mikel stumbled backwards as claws slashed past his face. "By the Gods!" He had felt the breeze of their passing.

The Chthonians were hidden themselves in hollows, blending in with the resinous material they had secreted to build their nest. Elongated heads appeared as the skeletally-thin bodies uncurled and took nightmarish shape. Double-jaws gaped open in soft hisses.

"I claim blood-debt!" Norvgan charged forward and swung his axe with an eager shout.

"Have at thee!" Mikel sliced his sword through the thin neck of one demon and hastily ducked the spray of acidic greenish blood.

Geoff raised his staff. "I banish thee!" he intoned in a cold tone of voice. Lightning flashed down the tunnel.

"There's too many of them!" Gavin called out as more of the creatures appeared out of hiding.

"I know that!" Geoff flung another lightning bolt. "I know!" A drop of icy cold liquid fell onto his hand and he looked up.

A double-jawed mouth gaped open as the demon hissed.

The Chthonian dropped from the ceiling to land on the floor with a soft thud. It hissed again. A claw slashed out and snapped the mage's staff in half with a spray of sparks.

Geoff stared in horror at the broken wood in his hand. "My staff!" he cried. "My staff!"

The demon hissed and took a step closer.

Geoff backed away.

An arrow hissed past Geoff's ear to catch the demon in its elongated head and it toppled over and fell to the floor.

"We can't hold them for long."

"There's too many of them!" Gavin shrieked as clawed hands reached for him. "Help!"

"Gavin!" Mikel swung around and hacked desperately with his sword. An arrow flashed past his shoulder to strike a Chthonian.

A demon lashed out and pulled an archer into an alcove. The man screamed in horror.

Norvgan hacked down another Chthonian. "No honour, just blood!" he grunted. "'Tis not battle, 'tis vermin control." He swung at another demon. "Mage!"

Geoff was kneeling on the floor, staring at his broken staff.

"Geoff!" Norvgan bellowed.

Mikel hacked at an skeletal arm with a snarl.

A demon approached the mage, its whip-like tail swishing violently from side to side.

"Get away from me!" Geoff swung his fist and bluish lightning flared from his empty hand.

The Chthonian shrieked as lightning played across its bluish-green body. It bent low, giving its head a shake and the lashing of its tail increased. Double jaws snapped as it advanced once against towards the mage.

"Get away!" Geoff gestured again and fresh lightning crackled across the demon's carapace.

Mikel stared at the smoking corpse in wide-eyed shock—the other Chthonians were either dead or else they had vanished. "I thought thy staff was broken."

"It is." Geoff stared down at the splintered ash. "But somehow I no longer have need of it." He smoothed out his tunic and stood straighter. "I have moved beyond the crutch." He sounded a little surprised.

Gavin was keeling beside one of his guardsmen. "Damn it all." Half of the man's face was simply gone.

"Only the greatest of mages ever become accomplished at casting with a staff or other prop." Norvgan gave the blade of his axe a careful study. "'Tis no small feat to master, let alone accomplish in the heat of battle."

Geoff said nothing.

Mikel nodded his head once. "Fine...let's see thou if thou can keep up with the tricks."

"Do we all still stand?" Norvgan asked.

Gavin shook his head. "They took Kurt and Heinrich. Jaime is dead. Damn them."

Mikel cursed. "The black powder?"

"Gone."

"Damn it." Mikel clutched the hilt of his sword more tightly.

"Then we must do this without the powder." Geoff sighed loudly, then stood more straight and squared his shoulders. "Follow me." He set off down the tunnel, his torn cloak fluttering behind him.

· Chapter Twenty-One

Geoff stood in front of another corpse. This one was laying on the floor, against the wall, his body burned, black and crisp, his skeletal face contorted in obvious agony. The ruby ring on his hand shone dully.

"Another victim?"

"My Master. 'Tis my master." Geoff reached out and lightly brushed his fingers against his master's cheek. "I found him down here." His voice was quiet, a light flickering in his eyes. "I had been curious about his experiments and his reliance upon total secrecy. Even the servants had noted his growing obsession with this lowermost level. One man had been exiled from the tower after supposedly venturing below. 'Dismissed for theft,' or so Conrad had claimed when Jurgen failed to serve at breakfast. Though now I can only wonder....

"Curiosity is a terrible weakness of mine. It has brought me knowledge and learning, but it has cost me many sleepless nights. Even in my youth before I learned the magical arts and delved too deeply into what is rightfully forbidden knowledge.

"I followed Conrad down into the cellar that last night. I followed him through the corridors, shrouded from discovery by a spell I had only recently learned, until he reached this spot. This is where the secretions first began to appear." He tapped the material covering the walls. "Before they spread so far. This is where he began to murmur a spell.

"And then the Chthonian appeared, uncoiling itself from the very wall." A flush coloured Geoff's cheeks. "I fainted."

Norvgan chuckled.

Mikel and Gavin exchanged looks.

"I do not know how long I slumbered here, but I remained hidden by my magic. I awoke, half inside one of these alcoves. I was terrified. Terrified of what I had seen. Of what Conrad might do should he discover me. I tried to leave, tried to find my way back to the surface but it was all quite impossible. I was disoriented and the foul scent of this place was overpowering.

"And I was afraid of encountering another demon."

"There is no fear in that, lad."

"I had seen the way the first one simply unfolded itself from the wall. How many more might be hiding in plain sight?" Geoff gestured absently towards the walls. "How many might be watching me right then? Ready to pounce the moment I moved." He whirled on his heel. "How could I dare to move when they might strike?" His hand brushed the body and bits fell loose to scatter across the floor. "Nor could I cower there for long...for how much longer might my spell conceal me?" Geoff voice was soft. "I had thought my master was experimenting with dragons...not with these demonic creatures."

Mikel nodded.

"I wandered aimlessly in the tunnels for a time, going in circles for it was a maze even then, before I turned a corner and there stood my master. Conrad glared at me..."

"Thou dare trespass within my innermost sanctum?" Conrad's voice echoed through the corridors.

"I'm sorry, master." Geoff bowed low, the hem of his robe rubbing in the dirt. "I didn't mean anything."

"Sneaking wretch! The secrets I have chosen to share were not enough for thee? Thou need to steal more knowledge from me?" Conrad raised his arm and the ruby ring on his hand glittered.

"No, Master!" Geoff cried out.

Conrad turned away. "I will have thou banished beyond the barony for this. No mage will ever again talk to thee. Ye shall be outcast and exiled."

"No, Master." Geoff crawled across the floor. "Please, show me mercy for I am loyal to thee."

"Wretch, ye would ask me for—gah!" Conrad doubled over with a cry.

"Master?"

"I-I am fine." He straightened, the fury fading from his face to be replaced with one of serenity. "I have communed with the Mother and she has blessed me with the greatest mystery of divine life." He took a deep breath, his expression darkening once again. "Thou could also have shared such knowledge...had thou not proven thyself to be treacherous."

"I'm sorry, Master. I would never steal from you."

"Lies!" Pain twisted Conrad's face. "Lies!"

Something hissed in the shadows.

"I would have thou exiled, but that fate is too kind for thee." A smile played across his face. "Perhaps thou should be taken to the Mother."

"What Mother?" Geoff asked blankly.

Another hiss came from behind him.

Geoff turned. "By the Gods! What manner of dragon is this?"

The bluish-green demon opened its inner set of jaws and hissed. Thick clear slime dripped from its fangs onto the flagstones. Its elongated head swung from side in a slow, sinuous movement.

"Thou were not worthy." Conrad shook his head with great sadness. "Thou are weak."

The skeletally-thin demon reached towards Geoff with a claw-tipped hand.

Conrad coughed into his hand. "Perhaps the Mother will find some worth in thee...or perhaps she will merely dine on thy bones." He coughed again. "I leave the choice to her."

"Please, don't do this!"

"Thou could have had greatness." Conrad stopped to gasp for breath. "Thou are a great failure." He doubled over. "By the Gods!" He clutched at his chest, his face contorting. "By...the...Gods!"

Geoff's eyes widened.

Blood was staining the chest of Conrad's blue tunic.

The mage's mouth opened in a scream.

The demon hissed as it watched.

"Master!" Geoff screamed and reached desperately towards the old man.

"I don't know what happened next," Geoff muttered. "There was fire and thunder and then everything simply went black."

"Thou survived."

"I came to my senses in Beaudral. A bed in the inn. Apparently I had been found wandering naked in the forest after a fierce storm."

Mikel smiled down at Conrad. "At least he got what he deserved."

"A just punishment," Gavin agreed. "For consorting with demons."

"What's that?" Norvgan bent down to pick something from the floor. "'Tis a ring."

Geoff turned. "His ring!" He reached for it. "I will take that." He grabbed it and clenched it tightly within his hand.

"His ring?"

Geoff nodded. "It was a focal point for his magic. It can become mine. Such is the right of mages." He slid the ring on his finger where it shone dully.

"And now what?"

"Now we venture deeper still. We are near the heart of the tower." Geoff sighed, almost in rapture. He was staring into the distance. "I can sense the flow of magical energies. I can almost *see* them in the air. We are near the very centre of the maelstrom." He touched the wall for a moment. "Can't thou feel it?" he asked. "Pulsating around us."

"Feel what?"

"The current of magic."

Gavin frowned. "Mage, don't go mystical on us now. We need thou to stay focused."

Geoff sighed. "Yes, of course." He shook his head. "Conrad designed this place to *aid* in his studies. It helps to focus the currents of magic." He shook his head again. "But it was never this strong before. I'm sure of that fact. No, 'twas never this strong."

"So those creatures are truly magical?"

"Possibly. They certainly are not of this world."

"Now which way?"

Geoff gestured ahead to an archway. "Through that archway. That should be the heart."

The chamber beyond was dimly lit, the torches almost completely obscured beneath the resin coiled over the wall.

"What are those?" Mikel gestured to the barrel-sized objects which dotted the floor. There were dozens of them.

"Eggs, I dare say." Geoff narrowed his eyes at the leathery objects. "Yes, definitely eggs. Larger than the one the cult had, but they looked similar."

Something hissed in the dim shadows of the room.

"Stay close." Mikel gripped his sword.

Norvgan grunted. "Ye need not tell me."

"Do not venture close to the eggs." Geoff shook his head, though a smile played across his lips. "No chicken will hatch from any of them."

Another hiss echoed from the shadows.

"By the Gods!" Norvgan swore.

The creature which loomed over them truly was a demon from the lowest depths of the Inferno. It was three or four times the height of a man, vaguely humanoid, with an extra set of claw-tipped arms sprouting from its chest. The head was elongated even more, with a horn-like frill topping it. her chitinous body was more green than blue.

"It's their queen." Mikel stared at the beast.

Geoff took a deep breath. "By all the Gods."

"We have to kill it." Gavin lifted his bow and loosed an arrow.

The arrow flew and bounced from the queen's head.

She hissed, opening her double jaws.

Gavin knocked another arrow.

"Her natural armour is too strong for thou to harm." The mage gestured, waving them back. "This must be fought with magic." He made a throwing motion with his hand and lightning lashed out from his fingers.

The queen shrieked.

Mikel winced. "We're just making her mad!"

"Have at ye!" Norvgan charged at her with his axe raised.

The queen's bony tail lashed out and sent him flying into the wall. He fell to the floor and lay unmoving.

Two Chthonians hissed as they scuttled through a narrow tunnel and into the chamber.

"They're mine!" Gavin fired a last arrow, then drew his sword and charged at the pair. "Take the queen!"

Mikel feinted with his sword and dodged the slash of her tail even as Geoff lashed her with more of his lightning. "She's too fast!" His sword struck her leg, but failed to cut through. "We're not going to be able to take her down."

"We must!"

"We're not even hurting her!" Mikel threw himself clear as a clawed arm lashed at him.

"I know." Geoff was panting. "Even with the magical currents being focused in this room, I am nearing exhaustion." He shook his head. "My spell is having little effect on her armour."

The queen screeched. She loomed over them, his tail lashing.

"How the hell do we slay such a beast?" Mikel demanded.

Gavin cut down the last Chthonian and turned back towards the queen. "Three against one. An ending worthy of song."

"Who will record such a song?" Geoff shouted back over the shrieks of the demonic queen.

"Whomever of us lives?"

"The casks." Mikel gestured with his sword. "Over there!" The casks of black powder were there, on the floor beside the bodies of two guardsmen.

"Heinrich! Kurt!" The two men were bound nor restrained in any apparent manner. "Are they still alive?"

"Are they infected?" Mikel asked.

"Surely there's not been enough time for that to have happened." Gavin shook his head. "We have to get them clear."

"How?"

Gavin opened his mouth, then closed it again. "I don't know," he admitted sourly.

"Get yourselves clear." Geoff wiped blood from his forehead. "Get the Dwarf." He hurled another lightning bolt at the queen who shrieked back.

"But what about you?"

"Don't worry about me, Mikel. Get the Dwarf away."

Mikel cursed and ran to Norvgan's side.

Gavin reached for his bow again. "I can help distract her!"

"There is no time!" Geoff stepped towards the queen. "No time."

The queen hissed and loomed even taller.

"Ye Gods." Mikel reached the Dwarf's side. "He's still breathing." He froze as the queen hissed and took a step toward him. "Damn it!"

"Leave them alone!" Geoff hurled a lightning bolt and one of the leathery eggs blew apart in a spray of yellow-green goo.

The queen shrieked.

Gavin stumbled.

Mikel clutched at his ears. His head was ringing.

"Did ye not like that?" Geoff shouted. "I can do it again."

The queen turned back towards him, mouth gaping open in a hiss.

"Gavin!" Mikel dragged Norvgan's towards the entrance, cursing the Dwarf's surprising weight. "Come on!"

Gavin cursed, but retreated towards the archway. He never took his eyes from the queen, but she was ignoring him now for the mage.

Geoff sidestepped and the queen matched his movement.

Mikel and Gavin reached the archway. "We're clear, fall back with us Mage!" They kept hurrying backwards, heading towards safety.

"For all those poor souls that thou has slain," Geoff said as he stared directly into the queen's nonexistent eyes, "I banish thee back to the Inferno!" He threw a final lightning bolt.

Mikel heard the thunderous boom and a cloud of smoke billowed up the tunnel, surrounding him with foul-smelling vapours. Rocks fell from the ceiling, bouncing off them hard enough to leave bruises.

Norvgan coughed and opened his eyes. "Ye Gods," he muttered. "What happened?"

Gavin was still coughing.

Mikel closed his eyes for a moment. "I think Geoff just killed the Mother." He reopened his eyes and looked down the tunnel. "And it cost him his life."

Norvgan shook his head. "Gods."

Discover other titles by Matt Kirkby at Smashwords.com:
Connect with Me Online:
Smashwords: http://www.smashwords.com/profile/view/MattKirkby
Facebook: http://facebook.com/MattKirkby
Facebook Fan-Page: Matt Kirkby's Facebook fan page

Also by Matt Kirkby

A Novel of Lovecraftian Horror
The Death of Hope

Standalone
A Wyrm In the Heart
Cthonian Dragons
The Horror From The Sea

About the Author

Born and raised in small-town Ontario, Matt Kirkby is a romantic dreamer who specializes in writing tales of high fantasy and pulp-style science fiction and space operas. He draws his inspiration from all diverse sources and ideas: Science Fiction, Fantasy, Gothic Horror, Pastoral Nature. He started his writing career submitting fan fiction for numerous Star Wars and TransFormers fanzines, but has since moved on to writing professionally. He published his first novel, A Wyrm In The Heart in 2004. He lives a double life, writing classy sci-fi and fantasy for fun under his own name, and penning gay erotica under the pen name of Frank Sol. When not writing, Matt spends his time helping his partner with his hand-crafted rocking chair business -- www.OffYourRocker.ca -- and trying to maintain some control over his cat. He still thinks that no gift is better than a new book.

www.ingramcontent.com/pod-product-compliance
Lightning Source LLC
Chambersburg PA
CBHW021219170726
47994CB00013BA/474